AN ALL NEW
SECRET AGENT "X" ANTHOLOGY
Volume Four

SECRET AGENT "X"

Mountain Men *of the* Lost Valley

by Bobby Nash

Alexander Lienen sidestepped a hail of bullets.

But only just by centimeters.

Rounding a corner into what he believed to be an empty hallway, he was surprised to find a squad of Soviet soldiers standing there. Equally surprised, the soldiers opened fire without a word.

Why are they here? he wondered.

Are they on to me?

The man who had presented himself weeks before as an observer sent by Moscow to oversee operations at The Citadel in the Ukrainian city of Kiev, Lienen had full access to all areas involved in matters of scientific research. However, the section of the Citadel where he currently found himself was strictly off limits to all except the military.

Alexander kept mental note of the time.

There was precious little of it remaining, he knew. He had calculated every detail down to the last possible second. However, running afoul of a squadron of Moscow's finest soldiers who were not where they were supposed to be was not something he had factored. Soviet soldiers were generally more regimented. It was unlike them to be in the wrong position. Then again he wasn't exactly supposed to be there, either, so who was he to throw stones.

Timing was critical and the countdown was quickly descending. Slipping two small capsules from inside a small pouch hidden in his belt, he gave them each a small squeeze, breaking the thin membranes that kept the two liquids inside separated.

Counting to three he tossed the capsules around the corner at the oncoming guards and quickly pulled back as more bullets pelted the stone wall just above his head, shredding to confetti. If nothing else, he had to respect their aim.

A small puff echoed in the tight confines of the concrete corridor as the first capsule ruptured, releasing its contents into the air. As the liquids combined they immediately altered from separate inert materials into a potent paralytic gas. It took only a couple of seconds for the gas to expand beyond the capsules' ability to hold it.

He smiled as he heard the second puff of gas being ejected into the air as the remaining capsule popped.

Pulling a handkerchief from his jacket pocket, Alexander Lienen

THE MAN OF A THOUSAND FACES

Airship 27 Productions

SECRET AGENT X: VOLUME FOUR
An Airship 27 Production

MOUNTAIN MEN of the LOST VALLEY © 2012 Bobby Nash
DOCTOR FEAR © 2012 Jarrod Courtemanche
A STYGIAN UNKINDNESS © 2012 Kevin Noel Olson
CROWN of the COBRA KING © 2012 Frank Schildiner

Editor: Ron Fortier
Associate Editor:Ray Riethmeier

Cover © copyright 2012 Shane Evans & Rob Davis
Interior illustrations © copyright 2012 Rob Davis

Production and design by Rob Davis

Published by Airship 27 Productions
airship27hangar.com

ISBN-13: 978-0615710778
ISBN-10: 0615710778

Printed in the United States of America

10 9 8 7 6 5 4 3 2 1

chanced a glance around the corner. As he suspected, the guards had been incapacitated by the gas and were lying unconscious on the cold stone floor. They would survive, although they would wake in a few hours with among the worst headaches of their lives.

Moving quickly through the gas, his mouth and nose covered by the cloth kerchief, Lienen stopped long enough to pull a pistol from the holster of one of the unconscious soldiers who had no use for it at the moment.

Armed, he resumed his course.

Timing was critical.

Ahead of him was freedom.

Behind him all hell was about to break loose.

And when it did he planned to be far, far away.

A shouted command from somewhere ahead brought him to a complete stop. More soldiers were coming up the stairs at the far end of the corridor. He could see their shadows stretching up the uneven concrete wall like specters rising from the earth in search of some unsuspecting innocent soul.

Alexander considered himself many things, but innocent was not among them. One did not survive in his line of work without getting one's hands a little dirty. It came with the job.

The stairwell option was no longer open to him. Unfortunately, it had been his only viable means of escape.

He needed a new plan.

And he needed it fast.

Quickly surveying the area he noticed that the corridor had two windows set along the outer wall. They were the only source of illumination inside the stone hallway. Thankfully, they were hinged. That meant they could be opened from the inside, which meant he had a new plan. He tucked the gun into his belt and went over to the window.

Pushing the first window open, he looked down. It was easily a five hundred foot drop to the mighty Dneper River below. Without a parachute it was suicide to even attempt such a jump. With a chute the leap would have been a far easier feat.

Sadly, Alexander was short exactly one parachute.

The voice of the lead soldier grew closer. He could also hear the pounding of footfalls hitting the stone steps. They would be on him within seconds.

Alexander was out of time.

Taking a deep breath, he stepped onto the ledge and went out the window. Like most of the ancient buildings in the ancient city of Kiev, the Citadel was built more for defense than for aesthetics. The exterior was not flush, which left many potential handholds.

Holding tightly, he felt the sharp edge of the jagged creases in the stone cut into his fingers. He ignored the pain. With his foot he pushed the window closed. The last thing he needed was a curious soldier to wonder why the window was open and take a peek outside.

Off to his left was a stone section that angled down several hundred feet. He knew from his weeks in the Citadel that inside the section in question was a stairwell that led from the Citadel to several rocky outcroppings below. Beyond that was the boat dock and the sea plane berth.

The stairwell was not part of the original design, which was built primarily to keep attacking nomadic tribes at bay. The additional stairwells were added much later at the behest of the Russians when Kiev fell under Soviet jurisdiction. The Soviets had since taken the Citadel for their own use. It was rumored that they were experimenting with new technologies as part of a plan for expanding their Communist Empire.

Hand, toe, hand, toe, Alexander slowly made his way along the treacherous rock wall of the Citadel with the skill of a professional free climber—although he would not have turned down a harness and a rope had they been available. Hundreds of feet below him, the river waited. One wrong move, one misstep and the river would claim him as it had reportedly claimed so many others over the years.

He had no intention of allowing the river such satisfaction.

Finally reaching the top of the stairwell, Alexander managed to crabwalk slowly down the incline, which was steep, but manageable. Unfortunately, the going was far too slow. He was going to miss his rendezvous.

And there was the matter of the ticking time clock counting down in his brain.

Before making his escape, the man known as Alexander Lienen—a famed Russian scientist sent to inspect the Citadel facility—had broken into the office of the head of the project, one General Andre Suverov. It took a few moments, but he found what he was searching for, a magnetic tape with all of the top-secret details of the Citadel's experiments.

The tape was used to transmit data from the Citadel to Moscow. Once the tape reached its destination it would be fed into a magnetic recorder and decrypted. Then the person on the other end could read the information.

Alexander Lienen's job was to keep that information from reaching its target.

He slowly made his way along the treacherous rock wall of the Citadel

Mission accomplished.

Unfortunately, there was nothing to prevent a second tape from being created. Knowing that the experiments continued, there was only one course of action open to him. The experiments had to be destroyed.

Using his intricate knowledge of chemicals, he set in motion a reaction inside one of the more volatile experiments. As the liquids merged together inside the great machine, a chain reaction would build and build until finally destroying the secrets the Citadel held.

The experiments would be set back by decades or, best case scenario, they would be labeled a failure and scrapped completely.

With his act of sabotage behind him, and a chain reaction building far faster than he had minutes available, his energies were now fully focused on escape. He reached the bottom of the stairs without being spotted. There was only one guard standing by the door below him. Alexander knew it was standard procedure. His job was to control who went in and out of the door. The guard would not be expecting a visitor from above.

It was an easy matter to take out the guard with a simple jiu-jitsu strike to the back of the neck.

Alexander ran down the path toward the river docks. He knew there were several boats at the dock he could commandeer for his escape. Sometimes there were small seaplanes in the area, which would have been a better mode of escape, but there were no planes available to him at the moment.

A boat would suffice.

Reaching the dock, he took up position beside a tree and waited as his mental countdown reached zero.

Above, he heard the satisfying *boom!* of an explosion that he knew signaled the end of the Citadel's great machine. He listened carefully as several successive explosions ripped through the facility. The outer wall of the Citadel erupted as flame and smoke broke free from the confines of the laboratory and leapt skyward.

An alarm sounded.

He ducked behind a tree for cover as the guards on duty at the dock ran up the path. One man remained on watch while his companions went to investigate the explosion. Once they were out of sight, Alexander Lienen ran onto the dock.

The remaining guard pointed his gun at the new arrival. Panting and out of breath, the man's hands were bleeding and his face and clothes tinged with dirt, sweat, and blood. He coughed violently as he tried to catch his breath.

"What happened?" the guard shouted in his native tongue.

"Accident," Lienen answered in the same dialect, but with heavy breathing added for effect. "Explosion," he added with a cough. Distracted by his coughing, the guard did not see the gas pellet until it popped at his feet. By then it was too late. The guard crumpled to the wooden dock, unconscious.

It only took a moment to commandeer a boat, disable the remaining ones, and to blast away from the dock toward the rendezvous. Once far enough away that he knew no one was following him, Alexander Lienen scratched at his neck, tugging at the skin until it began to peel away beneath his fingertips.

Seconds later Alexander Lienen was no more.

In his place stood the man known only as X.

X pulled a small vial from his pocket and sprayed it onto the mask of Lienen's face, which began melting as the spray hit it. Satisfied that there would be no proof that Alexander Lienen had been anywhere near Kiev, X tossed the disintegrating mask into the Dnieper River where it quickly sank beneath the waves.

He tapped his jacket pocket. The magnetic strip was safe. He knew that K-9 was anxious to get his hands on the information stored there.

Secret Agent X was simply anxious to get home.

X was tired.

It had been a long journey out of Kiev. He had taken the appropriated boat as far as he could before boarding a train that took him through Romania and into Hungary. Once in Hungary, a short hike took him to a small airfield where he booked passage as A.J. Martin of the Associated Press who was legally in the country on an assignment. That brought him to Switzerland where he spent the evening sitting on the balcony of a beautiful chalet looking out at one of the most picturesque views he had ever laid eyes on.

The Swiss Alps was breathtaking this time of year and X enjoyed the view. His only regret was that his ladylove, the equally breathtaking Betty Dale, was not there to share it with him. He missed the warmth of her sitting next to him in the chilled night air.

Perhaps one day, when his mission was done and the world no longer needed an operative such as Secret Agent X, perhaps he and Betty would vacation here. *Or perhaps even honeymoon,* he thought and smiled. X reveled in his romantic thoughts, knowing that despite how much he loved her, he could not marry Betty until he had rid the world of evil and corruption.

He had a long road ahead of him.

Thankfully, Betty's beauty was matched only by her patience. She would wait for him as long as it took. Not for the first time, the man known as Secret Agent X realized he was a lucky man.

At least he would only be in Switzerland for one night. A train was departing the next morning for France. From France, only a Trans-Atlantic flight stood between him and the home he missed. Despite the splendor of world travel, there was truly no place like the good ol' U. S. of A., and he could not wait to get back there.

But, like Betty, X was also patient.

He could hold out a few more days.

A quick shower later and A.J. Martin stepped out of the chalet into the softly fluttering snow. He felt the chill of the winter air even through the mask that disguised Secret Agent X as the world-renowned journalist.

As Martin, X took a leisurely stroll around the shops of the tourist village. He used various techniques to make sure no one was following him or watching him too closely. Satisfied that he was not under surveillance, X stopped to eat at a nice restaurant that also featured an exquisite view of the Alps in the not too far off distance. After enjoying the fine meal, Martin thanked the chef and stepped once more out into the cold. He cinched the scarf about him tighter, surreptitiously patting his jacket pocket and feeling relief that the magnetic strip was still safe and sound where he had left it.

That night X dreamt of mountain climbing. In his dream he and Betty Dale were alone on top of the world's largest mountains sipping champagne. She had packed a picnic lunch and he was there as himself, without a mask.

It was a nice fantasy.

But, like most pleasant dreams, it ended with the dawning sun.

That morning, A.J. Martin checked out of the chalet and took on the role of tourist, visiting shops of various interests. Should anyone have noticed the newspaperman in town this would add to the cover that he was simply on a sightseeing expedition, busy purchasing last minute gifts for the folks back home. In fact, he was making sure that no one was following him.

Later that afternoon, the Associated Press journalist boarded a train bound for France.

Having planned ahead, he requested a private car. Comfortable though he was in the persona of A.J. Martin, X knew that he had to spend some time each day as the man beneath the mask. It was important that he never forget his true identity.

The train left the station, surprisingly, on time. After making sure it was free of surveillance devices, A.J. Martin settled into his compartment and X enjoyed some much-needed solitude. No mask required. Alone in his cabin he did not need to play a role.

A few hours later, a refreshed A.J. Martin stepped into the dining car.

He sat alone and sipped on the steaming hot cup of coffee in front of him. The dining car was not full, a few other passengers sat and enjoyed casual conversation as they ate a small dinner. From overhearing bits and pieces of conversation going on around him, X knew that there was a doctor on vacation with his wife on board. There was also a student on sabbatical, a writer, and at least two people with vastly disagreeing philosophies on current events brewing in Germany who argued their various points of view over a friendly game of cards. The rest of the passengers were content to keep to themselves. A few were reading while one gentleman had nodded off after his meal and snored softly. One older lady in the back was knitting what appeared to be a very ugly sweater.

The train's course took them through a beautiful mountainous region and X was content to sit alone and enjoy the ride. Outside, a brilliant blanket of snow covered everything in a wintry coat, which sparkled under the full moon that sat atop a cloudless, star-filled night sky. The mountains looked purple under the bright moon.

"Beautiful, isn't it?" a mysterious voice asked.

"I beg your pardon?" X said, startled from his reverie.

"Sorry," the owner of the voice said. He held out a hand and introduced himself. "Pierre Michon."

"A.J. Martin," X responded instinctively. "A pleasure."

"Mind if I join you?" Michon asked.

"Not at all. Please." X motioned to the chair opposite him.

The newcomer eased himself into the chair stiffly. X noticed the movement of a man with a wooden leg, but did not draw attention to it. There were many who had suffered during the War. From his age, X presumed that Pierre Michon had seen action. Unfortunately, the world had not learned its lessons well. X knew that not too far from his very location a potentially cataclysmic situation was brewing.

Is another war on the horizon? he wondered, but just as quickly put the danger coming out of Nazi Germany from his mind. There would be time enough to dwell on those thoughts later. X had actually contemplated a side trip to Berlin while he was in the area, but decided it would be smarter to wait until he had reliable intelligence on the situation. He planned to ask K-9 to follow up on his concerns the next time he communicated with his handler.

"Would you like a cup?" X asked the newcomer, pointing to the coffee.

"Thank you."

The reporter motioned for the attendant, who nodded and brought over an extra cup and filled it for Michon.

"You can leave the pot," Martin said as he tipped the attendant, who left the steaming pot of coffee on the table. "So, what brings you to the Alps, Mr. Michon?"

The man smiled. Slightly drooped, the Frenchman spoke with a gruff voice that did not seem to fit his face. A scruffy white beard—one that matched the snowy wonderland on the other side of the window—covered scars. Yes, this man had seen his share of unpleasantness in the War.

Then again, so had the man called X.

"Work," the man answered with a grunt.

"Oh. What kind of work are you in, sir?"

"Courier. I oversee deliveries of various wines and desserts from France to some of the finest restaurants in all the world."

"That's very interesting," Martin said, resting his elbows on the table as he listened. "I had a fabulous French wine at the restaurant last night. Perhaps one of yours?"

"Possibly. Our vineyard produces some of the finest grapes in the country," he said proudly. "I routinely transport our vintage along this route."

"So you spend a lot of time on this route?"

"Oh, yes. This is my favorite leg of the trip."

"I can see why," Martin said. "This view is...."

"I know. Beautiful." He motioned toward the purple-hued mountains not far away.

"So, what kind of work do you do, Monsieur Martin?"

"I'm a reporter with the Associated Press."

That piqued his companion's interest, as was usually the case when A.J. Martin introduced himself. "Oh? And you are here on an assignment, yes?"

"No. Not really." Martin smiled softly as he leaned back in his chair. "I mean, a good reporter is always on the lookout for a good story, but right now I'm content to sit back and enjoy the ride."

"Well, you've picked a good time to take this trip, Mr. Martin. The view is even lovelier this time of year than usual."

"It is lovely," A.J. Martin agreed as he pointed out the window. "I've seldom seen such a sight."

"This area is commonly referred to as The Lost Valley."

"Really? That is interesting," the reporter said, leaning closer to the window for a better view. "Why do they call it that?"

"Well, legend has it that there are small encampments of men living out there who are so far removed from civilization that they can only be considered savages. Lost from civilization, they are rumored to live in the past."

"Savages?" Martin asked. "Like cavemen?"

"I cannot say, sir," Pierre said with a wry smile. "Personally, I have never seen them up close, but there have been stories of wild men and nasty savage beasts roaming the Lost Valley."

"Of course there have," X mumbled.

"Where I come from we have the legend of Big Foot. The back story seems somewhat similar," X said aloud.

"Possibly."

"Is there anything else of interest I should be on the lookout for?" he asked, genuinely curious.

"Oh, there is much to see. Why, I was just telling that young lady over there," he said as he waved at a dark haired young lady sitting at the rear of the dining car reading a worn pulp paperback novel.

X turned to follow the wave and saw as she returned it with a shy one of her own. X nodded a long distance greeting.

"Pretty girl."

"Indeed, sir," Michon said, a smile splitting his scruffy face. "I was telling the mademoiselle that we had a good chance of seeing the mountain men on this trip."

"Mountain men?"

"Yes, sir. The savages I mentioned. There are villages scattered throughout the mountains," Michon said matter of fact. "Some of these villages are so cut off from civilization that no one even knows where they came from. They probably think the train is some kind of mythical beastie or something."

"I see." Despite the many unusual things he had seen himself, even X was having difficulty swallowing the Frenchman's tall tale.

"Many have claimed to have seen hunting parties moving through the valley," the courier continued. "Obviously, they live off the land."

"And is there any actual proof that these villages exist?"

"If you look closely, you might just be able to pick out their campfires. Perhaps a waft of smoke."

"Uh huh."

"I am serious, sir. Take my words to heart, Monsieur Martin. Just be glad you are on this train and not out there in the wilds."

"Because of the mountain men?"

"Trust me. You are far safer on the train than out there," he pointed to the mountains at the edge of the Lost Valley.

"The terrain looks treacherous," X said.

"It is," Pierre confirmed, which the Agent found odd since the courier admitted he had never been into the Lost Valley.

"Heed my warning. If they could, the mountain men would kill us all."

X tried to put the mountain men out of his mind.

Despite the seriousness of his travelling companion's words, X found it rather dubious that there were uncivilized mountain dwellers living off the land that were so out of touch that they would be unfamiliar with the modern locomotive. Especially considering that this particular train made numerous regularly scheduled trips on this rail line right along the edge of their reported homeland.

Lost Valley or no, there was no way anyone in the area could miss the noise of the train passing by in the night, especially since the echoing noises bouncing off the sheer mountain face on the one side of the tracks.

X admitted there was a slim possibility that there could be those who did not know of the advances in technology used to make the train run, but he doubted there were many who saw it as a mythical beast of any kind.

Then again, had he not himself witnessed many things that beggared the imagination?

X decided that there was no sense worrying over it.

If the mountain men were real and they truly feared the iron beast, then they would in all likelihood leave it alone. The only enemies that concerned him at the moment were those of Soviet persuasion. He had scanned the train earlier and was certain that no one from the Citadel knew his current whereabouts or his identity.

Still, Secret Agent X had not survived this long by being careless.

It was prudent to make certain he had not been followed, so another search of the train was due—just in case—after making small talk in the dining car with a few of the patrons. This included the shy girl with the book, who turned out to be a writer herself. Her name was Anna and she was travelling throughout the region, writing about her travels in a notebook. He agreed to read a few pages at her prompting and was impressed with her skill with words.

Like most in her chosen profession, Anna was in search of a grand adventure.

Be careful what you wish for, the Agent thought, but did not say aloud.

He gave her one of his cards with the information for A.J. Martin of the Associated Press and told her to mail him some of her stories when she felt ready. If nothing else, he offered to read them and give her honest feedback. X also made it a point to introduce Anna to the writer whose conversation he had overheard earlier. His name was Phillipe. He thought that perhaps he could offer her some insights into her burgeoning career.

Satisfied that the conversation was running smoothly on its own, A.J. Martin politely excused himself and made his way to the dining car's rear exit.

X paused a moment between the cars and inhaled the crisp mountain air. It tasted so much sweeter here than it did in New York. Aside from the smoke pouring from the train's engine, there were no traces of anything unnatural in the air. Back home there were automobiles on every street choking out black smoke that threatened to overwhelm Mother Nature's natural scent.

And he couldn't wait to return home and breathe deeply.

That and the smell of Betty's sweet perfume made him ache for home.

He lingered only a moment, feeling the chill creep over him before moving on to the next car. Like the dining car before it, this one was also sparsely populated. Four passengers were sleeping in their respective seats, with blankets pulled tightly around them. In the dim light, two older gentlemen were playing checkers on a tattered board, using light and dark colored beans as pieces. One of the players had just accused the other of cheating as X entered.

"How do you cheat at checkers?" the other man protested, his voice barely above a hushed whisper, which prompted a grin from X's alter ego.

The Agent passed through the car quickly without interrupting the game. There were only two other cars to check.

X stepped into the baggage car and froze.

The car was bathed in darkness, with the bright light from the full moon shining through the slats at the top of the car and from the partially open sliding door providing the room's only illumination.

Secret Agent X did not need his eyes to tell him something was amiss. He felt it as soon as he entered the room.

He was not alone in the baggage car.

There were three, no—four of them. In the dim moonlight he could just make out their outlines, but not their features. They were bulky, draped in thick coats made of various furs and animal skins. They were also easy to pick out by the musky smell, a mixture of smoke, sweat, and wet animal hair.

Mountain men? X wondered, suddenly giving more credence to the courier's story than he had previously. If they were these mountain men of which Pierre Michon had spoken, what was their interest in the train? Obviously, they were not as afraid of the mythical beast as he had been led to believe.

The intruders were rummaging through the baggage, careful to remain quiet, but not to hide their presence. Luggage was strewn across the floor, open suitcases hurled from one side of the boxcar to the other.

Focused as they were on their search, they had not heard him enter the car.

X decided to rectify the situation.

He cleared his throat loudly as he flipped on the light switch. The single bulb in the center of the car flared to life.

He had their attention.

"Excuse me, but would you care to explain what you're doing in here?"

Alerted to X's presence, the mountain men attacked.

With a snarl, the intruder nearest him launched himself at Secret Agent X.

In the cramped boxcar, surrounded by luggage and crates, X had nowhere to go. The mountain man, if that was indeed what his attacker was, packed quite a wallop. His bulky outerwear brilliantly disguised the mass of muscle that slammed into X.

They fell to the floor in a tangle of arms and legs.

X recovered quickly. With a powerful kick he pushed the savage away from him. X reacted instinctively, his extensive training taking over. He rolled away from the attack and was back on his feet in a shot.

Nearby, the stunned mountain man was getting up as well.

Unfortunately, X assumed his friends were not going to learn from his mistake and stand down.

He guessed correctly.

The three burly men advanced as one. X lanced out with a right, landing the heel of his palm in the chest of one of them. Before the other two knocked him off balance he heard the man gasp for air before collapsing. Outnumbered, X once again found himself on the floor in a tangle of limbs and wet, smelly animal skins.

The Agent struggled against the mountain men as they dragged him roughly to his feet.

"Last chance," X said. "Ready to surrender?"

The mountain man grunted a dismissive laugh.

"Okay. Don't say I didn't warn you."

The mountain men had numbers on him, but X had beaten heavy odds before. He brought down his heel heavily on the foot of the man on his right. Caught completely unaware by so simple a tactic he released his grip on the Agent's right arm.

X seized the opportunity and landed an uppercut under his captor's bearded chin with his now free hand. The mountain man flew backward and bounced off a stack of baggage that had not yet been searched before collapsing to the floor, buried under an avalanche of luggage.

Seeing an advantage, X planted his feet and launched himself backward. Like a battering ram he propelled the man holding him toward the wall behind them. With a satisfying crack, the mountain man released his grip on X.

One on one, it was an easy matter for X to take care of his attacker with a judo flip. The dazed mountain man hit the floor hard. X knew he would be seeing stars.

X spun, ready for the next attack.

The first man he fought squared off against him with a well-worn blade in his hand and a feral snarl on his lips.

"Look," X said as he took a step back, keeping just beyond the man's reach. "Why don't we discuss this like gentlemen?"

The mountain man lunged forward and X pivoted to the left so the slashing blade missed him. The man's aim was only off by centimeters as he cut the cloth of A.J. Martin's coat, but not the skin beneath it.

Off balance as the attack was, X had no trouble using the large man's momentum against him. A little push propelled the mountain man face first into the wall of the baggage car with a satisfying crunch followed by a thud as he dropped to the floor.

One of the big men managed a hard left jab that connected with X's jaw. The force of the blow sent X sprawling against the loading door. The door bucked and slid open, as it was no longer latched like it had been when they left the station earlier in the day. X felt the door slide open further under the impact. He saw blurred images of trees passing as the train hurtled along the track, oblivious to the life or death struggle taking place in the baggage car.

"Not bad," the Agent said as he steadied himself in the swaying car, the cold mountain air biting at his back. "I haven't taken a haymaker like that in quite some time."

The mountain man said nothing. His only reply was a series of deep, ragged breaths.

"Not much of a talker, are you?"

With a satisfying grunt, the mountain man produced a knife of similar design as the one his partner had used against X only moments before.

X clucked his teeth. "Well, at least you guys are consistent," he said. "I don't suppose you'd care to tell me what it is you're looking for in here, would you?"

The man slashed wildly with the knife. X pivoted to his left, sliding the door open even more. X felt the icy cold blast of air almost instantly numb his back.

"Somebody's going to get hurt if you keep this up," he warned.

His back to the far wall of luggage, X was cornered.

The three remaining mountain men advanced on him, each brandishing a knife. The Agent did not see too many appealing avenues of escape available.

"My mother used to say something that fits this situation," he said as his eyes darted across the room in search of anything to turn the tide of battle in his favor. X leapt upward and grabbed one of the luggage net hooks at the top of the car. Holding tightly he planted his foot in the face of one of his attackers, dropping him like a rock.

"It's only funny until someone loses an eye," he continued as he landed in a fighting posture.

The two remaining mountain men rushed him together.

X ducked under a slicing knife while landing a judo strike to the belly of his attacker. Unfortunately, countering both attacks at once wasn't easy and one of them got in a lucky shot.

A burning sensation flashed across X's leg where the attacker's knife had drawn blood. X saw brilliant flashes like a thousand flashbulbs exploding one after the other as the man he had evaded brought the hilt of his knife down on the back of the Agent's skull.

Still, X did not fall.

Drawing on his strength, X rose up beneath the man closest to him and lifted him from the floor only to drop him on his back. X landed atop the man, using his enemy's bulk to cushion the impact.

The room spun wildly around X from the blow to the head as he rolled off his fallen foe and got back on unsteady feet. From the man's brute strength, X felt fortunate that he was still awake to hear his heart thundering in his ears.

The Agent readied himself for the last attack. There was still one mountain man in fighting shape. *If only the room would stop spinning!* he thought just seconds before he caught sight of the attack.

X dove forward under the man's highhanded swing and caught him in an impressive tackle that would have done a professional football player proud. Unfortunately, X realized his miscalculation after his feet had left the floor.

There was a loud crack as both men hit the loading door, splintering wood under their impact.

Suddenly there was nothing beneath them as the door fell away. Secret Agent X and the mountain man fell from the speeding train to the waiting ground of the Lost Valley.

X hit the ground hard.

Remembering his combat training, he curled tightly and rolled upon impact. He could feel the freezing cold temperatures biting into his skin as he rolled through the rocks and snow. His leg burned from the knife wound.

He had lost sight of the mountain man as soon as they left the train. If his enemy recovered first then X was in trouble. He had to be the first one on his feet.

As it turned out, such considerations were unnecessary. X found the

There was a loud crack as both men hit the loading door, splintering wood under their impact.

mountain man's body near the spot where they had first impacted Mother Earth. Unlike X, his opponent had not known to tuck and roll.

"Guess you never had to jump out of an airplane before," X said as he looked down at the dead man at his feet.

Watching in silence, X shivered as the train continued on into the distance.

"This is certainly a fine mess," he said as he began stripping the animal skins from the dead mountain man's body.

"You'll forgive me," X told the corpse. "But I'm going to need these a lot more than you will."

Once he was sufficiently enmeshed in the smelly furs and leathers over A.J. Martin's expensive suit, X made his way back to the train tracks. He made sure that the magnetic tape was still safe and secure in its hiding place within the secret pocket hidden in the lining of his jacket.

Assured that the strip was safe, X stood in the center of the railroad track and surveyed his surroundings. The situation looked bleak. He blew out an exasperated breath as he looked toward the horizon as the train rounded the bend and disappeared from sight. This was not the best situation X had ever been in.

"Well, you've been in some tight spots before," he said to himself as he stared down the tracks. "I guess we're walking."

It would be easier to walk along the railroad timbers so he kept to the tracks where there was less snow build up, especially after the train's recent passage. This would prove helpful because the mountain man's animal skin boots had been too small for X's freezing feet.

Not knowing the lay of the land, it was best to stick to the tracks. It would be easy to walk into a hole filled with snow or to not see a sharp rocky outcropping. Plus, X knew the tracks led exactly where he needed to go.

"France," he whispered.

"I wonder how far away it is?"

As X walked along the darkened track he did not realize that he was not alone. There was something else out there in the eerie darkness of the Lost Valley.

Watching him.

And waiting.

X shivered from the cold.

By his estimation the temperature was holding steady just a degree or two above the freezing point. The heavy wind whipping around the sheer mountain face beside the railroad track made it feel considerably more frigid. The special materials used to make his masks often proved enormously helpful in the Agent's line of work. It helped him blend in. To infiltrate places like the Citadel they helped him become someone else entirely.

X had a newfound appreciation for the mask. It was a small layer of protection from the stinging snow against his skin. It wasn't much, but it might just stave off frostbite.

A short time later, X stopped. Fatigue tugged at him like a weight attached to his legs. The furs he had appropriated were as heavy as lead. His injured leg throbbed with each step. He let out a breath and saw the puff of warmth as it touched the wintry chill.

"Well, this is a fine pickle," A.J. Martin's voice said in his head.

"Y... you can say that again," X laughed, knowing he was talking to himself.

"What's that up ahead?" his alter ego asked.

"What?"

X looked ahead and he saw it.

"I... Is that...?"

"Light."

"But from what? Surely, the train hasn't stopped. Has it? Do they... Do they know I'm missing?"

"Only one way to find out."

"You're right," X whispered as he picked up his pace.

Pierre Michon stared out the window into the starry sky.

Ever since he had been a child he had loved winter. The snow, the wind, and that tingling feeling in his extremities that felt like pinpricks along his skin all made him feel more alive than any other sensation. He had taken the harsh punishment of Old Man Winter and had survived. As his father had said on many occasions, *"That which does not kill you will only make you stronger."*

It wasn't until he had answered his country's call and went to war that he learned the truth behind his father's words. When he had lost his leg, Pierre thought that his life was over. He could not conceive of any promising future for a one-legged man. Surely, there was no one who would hire a man with such a handicap when there were those whole of body to tackle the load.

But he had been mistaken.

A bona fide war hero, Pierre came home to several job offers, though none were to his liking. After a few years bouncing from one job he despised to another, Pierre struck upon a grand idea.

He would go into business for himself.

He did so and had become very successful.

As a courier, his record was exemplary.

"May I join you, Monsieur?"

Pierre looked up from his thoughts at the young woman he had been introduced to earlier as Anna.

"It would be my honor, mademoiselle," he said, rising unsteadily on his one good leg. "Please," he said as he pointed to the empty chair opposite him.

Anna dropped into the seat where the reporter had been sitting earlier.

"Would you care for something to drink?" he asked her.

"Thank you, but no," Anna answered. "I just wanted to sit by the window for a while if that is all right with you."

Pierre smiled. "Then you have come to the right place, mademoiselle. There is no more beautiful view that the one outside this window. Except, perhaps, the one sitting across the table from me."

Anna blushed and turned away to look out the window at the panoramic beauty of the snow covered land.

"Is this your first time in the valley?" Pierre asked, trying to turn the conversation to a topic less embarrassing for the girl.

"No." She answered so softly that the courier barely heard her.

Not wanting to upset her, he leaned closer to ask if she were okay.

He never got the chance.

Before he could open his mouth he heard a loud rumble. For a former soldier at war, the sound was unmistakable.

Explosion.

Before Pierre Michon could voice his concern, the train lurched forward as the engineer engaged the brakes, slowing the massive behemoth faster than its designers had intended. Plates, glassware, and eating utensils fell from their tabletop perches to the floor with a loud clatter. Passengers grabbed hold of whatever they could find for support. The train's lights dimmed, plunging the entire car into darkness.

Finally, the train eased to a stop.

"What's happening?" Anna asked as Pierre helped her back to her feet.

The lights came back on, but they were very dim, emitting just enough light to see the furniture and other passenger's positions.

Nervously, all eyes focused on the direction of the dining car's front door. If anyone was coming to explain, that is where it would happen.

"Why have we stopped?" Phillipe, the writer demanded.

Anna stiffened next to Pierre.

"What's wrong?" he asked.

"I'm scared."

"Stay here," he told her. "I'll go forward and see what's happening."

The courier took an uneasy step toward the door. He made it only halfway before the door burst open. In the open space stood a very large man dressed in burly furs and leathers.

"Oh no!" Pierre whispered as he skidded to a stop, grabbing a nearby table to keep himself upright. "Mountain men!"

The large man stepped into the car. His features were hidden by the dark, but there was no mistaking the aura of menace that surrounded him.

"I knew it!" Pierre whispered as he positioned himself in front of the young lady, urging her to walk backward away from the intruder.

When the mountain man finally spoke, his voice was rough and gravelly.

"You have something that belongs to us," he said.

"And we want it back!"

X could not believe his ears.

The Agent was no stranger to battle. One of the talents that he had perfected since the earliest days of the War was a discerning ear. Nine times out of ten X was successfully able to identify a gun from the unique sound each weapon emitted when fired. This skill had come in handy on several occasions. Just last year it had helped him clear the name of a friend that had been framed for the murder of a Federal City judge.

When he heard the explosion echo through the Lost Valley he knew something was wrong. At first X had thought the sound he heard was thunder, but when he heard a second blast he realized it for what it was.

It was the unmistakable sound of dynamite detonating.

The sound came from ahead, from around the same bend where the train had gone.

"That doesn't bode well," X whispered.

It was unlikely that someone who had legally boarded the train at the station had carried sticks of dynamite aboard.

Of course, the Agent was all too aware that there were people on the train who had not boarded at the station.

X picked up his pace and hurried toward the sound.

"So much for mindless savages," he said.

X spotted the train.

Surprisingly, it had stopped on the tracks just around the bend. He stopped to catch his breath and leaned against a long dead tree that remained standing only because it was frozen in place by the severe cold of the Lost Valley.

This was good news for the Agent. The train was a refuge from the wintry cold that surrounded him. He could no longer feel the tips of his fingers or his toes. He had to get inside soon or else he would not survive.

The train was undamaged from the initial look of it.

X assumed that the explosion had caused something to fall across the tracks in front of the train to block its path and keep it in place. There did not seem to be a similar blockage at the rear of the train, but since the conductor had not reversed course, X had to assume that someone—or more appropriately, a group of someones—had taken control of the engine car.

"Mountain Men," X whispered. It was the only explanation that made any kind of sense, though he honestly could not find much about the situation that truly seemed rational.

Obviously, Pierre Michon's claim that the mountain men were little more than savages left behind by the advance of civilization had not been entirely accurate. The men X had tussled with in the baggage car might not have been a very articulate bunch, but they knew enough about the modern world to work a suitcase.

And they had not been afraid of the train, as had been speculated. That much was certain since they had somehow managed not only to board the moving steam engine, but also to ransack the baggage car without being spotted.

If X hadn't interrupted their search when he had, who knew what might have happened next.

And now they had the train.

X wanted to know why they were after the train and what they were after. It was clear that they were searching for something in the baggage car. Something specific from the way they were frantically tearing through everything in the baggage car.

Obviously, they haven't found what they were looking for, X thought. *Otherwise there would have been no reason to stop the train.*

While he was still certain that this in no way had to do with his mission in the Ukraine, he could not dismiss the notion completely. As slim a possibility as it was, the mountain men could have been working for the Soviets. Or perhaps they were bounty hunters. Anything was possible and the Agent would not dismiss any notion until he was one hundred percent certain.

Careful not to alert anyone to his approach, X moved gently through the snow, which crunched softly beneath his feet. He hoped it did not sound as loud to others as it did in his ears where each step sounded like a thunder crack. He prayed no one inside could hear him.

Surprise was his only ally. No one knew he was off the train except the men he had tussled with in the baggage car and they would have assumed he was dead from the fall. Or, if he had managed to survive that, the elements would have surely made short work of him without proper protection.

But these mountain men did not know Secret Agent X.

He needed to keep his survival a secret until he was ready to make his move. Then, he would happily introduce himself to the Mountain Men of the Lost Valley.

As X reached the rear of the train he ducked beneath the balcony that hung off the end of the final car, which was also the car where those who worked the railways slept. X hoped it was empty.

He stayed crouched there for a moment and listened. He heard nothing. No one spoke. He did not even hear the crunch of snow underneath boots. He was alone. The mountain men had not spotted him.

X pulled himself onto the balcony quickly, using the rail instead of the steps. He paused at the door and listened. No sounds came from inside. The door's window was covered by a curtain on the inside and by a sheen of frost from the cold outside. X could not see any movement inside.

He gripped the door handle and gave it a slight tug.

The door did not move.

"Locked," X grunted softly as he pulled the magnetic strip from inside his inner jacket pocket. The strip slid easily in the space between the door and the frame that held it. He lifted the strip until it connected with the latch. With a quick thrust, the door unlatched and popped open.

X hurried inside and gently closed the door behind him. He returned the magnetic strip to its hiding place before taking another step.

The train car was dark save for the dull orange glow from the wood stove in the center of the room. It was just enough light to show X that the car was empty.

X warmed himself by the fire as he gave the room a quick look, taking inventory of what was available to him.

There wasn't much.

The room had a lived-in look, which translated to clutter. There were two sets of bunks mounted to the walls of the car. Four beds. There was not much else that X could possibly use to his advantage. X was not completely weaponless. He always carried a small selection of specialized gas pellets securely in his padded belt. His gas gun, however, was safely locked away in his cabin with his other belongings.

The Agent planned his next move as feeling returned to his extremities. The first order of business was dealing with his injuries. He ripped one of the bed sheets into strips and bandaged the knife wound in his leg. The wound had stopped bleeding while he had been walking through the cold outside. As he warmed, it once again began oozing crimson.

Step one in any potential hostage situation was reconnaissance. He would have to find out how many of these so-called mountain men were aboard and where they were stationed. His previous encounter with the mountain men told him that they were the strong, silent type.

Plus, in their multi-layered skins and thick beards, they were virtually identical to one another. That was definitely an advantage, considering he was already wearing the perfect disguise.

X pulled up the hood on his skins. The worn leather was hard and coarse as it rubbed against his skin, but that was a small price to pay. The disguise worked well enough. He did not have a beard like the others he had encountered, but that was easily disguised by pulling up the skins so they obscured his mouth and nose. The Agent's dirt-splattered, sweaty face was all but unrecognizable in his mountain man suit.

"Well, let's hope it fools the actual mountain men," X whispered as he opened the door and stepped between the cars.

He barely felt the cold this time, but moved quickly to the next car anyway. Now that he was warm he wanted to remain that way.

Taking a deep breath, Secret Agent X stepped into the baggage car.

The baggage car was cold.

X was not surprised since the train car no longer had a sliding cargo door that could be closed to keep out the elements. He moved silently through the carnage left behind by the mountain men's earlier search. Stepping cautiously over the scattered contents of the luggage, X headed for the door.

As he reached the far end of the car, X noticed the body of the mountain man he had slammed face first into the wall during the fight. He knelt next to the man and reached his hand into the skins covering his head to feel for a pulse.

There was none.

X did not enjoying killing. There was nothing as soul searing as taking a life. Unfortunately, in his line of work that was one of the unfortunate possibilities. Secret Agent X always looked for a way to stop his foes without resorting to killing, but sometimes there was no other choice.

X remembered the face of every man he ever killed.

He pulled back the skins and got a good look at the mountain man's face. His black hair was long and wild, as though it had never been introduced to a comb. His thick matted beard matched the color of the hair on his head, but was also streaked with gray. X guessed his age as somewhere in his mid to late forties, maybe early fifties from the wrinkles that were evident on his rough-hewn face.

X searched the deceased's body until he found what he was looking for. He pulled the knife and the pouch that held it from the mountain man's rope belt and attached it to his right wrist so the knife could easily be slid into his palm. The weapon might come in handy later, X believed.

Now armed and disguised, X made his way forward.

He stopped at the door to make sure there were no guards waiting between the cars. There were none so he eased himself out of the baggage car and quickly stepped over to the next car, a passenger car.

This car was empty as well. X remembered that passengers had occupied the room earlier. Most had been sleeping, except for the two gentlemen dueling over a checkerboard.

"They must have been moved to another car," X whispered as he slowly moved through the car to verify that it was indeed unoccupied. It was.

Alone in the passenger car, X thought he understood what was happening. The mountain men obviously did not outnumber the passengers so they had all been taken to a central location and guarded while the others searched for whatever it was that had brought them to the train.

X still had no idea what they could be looking for, but he suspected it was very important to them, enough so that they had made the attempt on a moving train.

X exited the baggage car and huddled by the door to the dining car. He could hear hushed voices talking inside. He assumed this was where the mountain men had sequestered the passengers.

Freeing the prisoners was important, but X needed to know how many intruders were on the train first. He needed to bypass the dining car and search the other cars. He needed to reach the engine car as well. Once he took care of the mountain men aboard he would have to make sure the train could move.

And there was also the matter of whatever had been dropped on the tracks ahead of them that caused the conductor to stop the train. He still had no idea what waited for him there. If it were a tree or boulder there was hope. If the explosion he had heard was the result of someone bringing down the entire side of the mountain that rose up beside the tracks then there was nowhere for them to go except back the way they came. Neither of which was the most appetizing of options for X.

Getting to the front of the train wasn't going to be easy. As near as he could tell there were three courses he could choose from.

He could take the high road and climb to the top of the boxcar and leapfrog his way to the front of the train while hoping no one spotted or heard him. It was a risky plan. The whipping wind could just as easily knock him off balance as it was as likely that someone inside would hear him. He scratched that option off as a no.

He could take the roundabout approach and circumvent the train on the ground. As with plan A, plan B was not without risks of its own. First, he would be back outside, which was not the smartest place to be when temperatures were hovering as close to the freezing mark as they were at the moment. Plus, X had no way of knowing how many mountain men were outside the train. This was their home turf and they had an advantage by knowing the terrain far better than he did. He marked this option as a maybe. If worse come to worst, outside was better than taking the high road.

His only other course of action was to boldly march right into the dining car and hope his disguise passed muster with the locals and the passengers. This plan was more in keeping with Agent X's usual method. His mountain man garb was just another mask, another role to play.

Plus, he had the distinct advantage that no one really knew him here. Oh, he had certainly talked to some of the passengers as A.J. Martin, but that was far different from trying to use a disguise on someone whom he saw and spoke to him daily like Detective John Burks. X hoped that one day he could tell the detective the truth just to see the look on his face when he learned the truth.

"Plan C it is," X whispered as he arranged the animal skin in a manner that would best hide his features.

Just in case, he told himself.

He twisted the handle slowly and relief washed over him like the rising tide when the latch turned. As silent as possible, X opened the door and eased inside the dining car. He felt the familiar warmth of the room even through his winter clothing. The passengers were sitting at the tables throughout the dining car. Three mountain men were walking back and forth through the room. Though they did not carry anything that resembled guns, they were armed.

X noticed an ax in one of the guard's hands. The second carried what looked like a large walking staff. The final guard had a sword tied to his back and held a mallet in his left hand that he kept slapping into his right. Clearly, of the three he was the most impatient which made him the most dangerous.

None of the pleasant conversation or friendly debates that filled the dining car earlier in the evening was present. The passengers were quiet. The silence of the room was deafening. One of the passengers sniffled and X assumed that at least one of the women had been crying, but he could not tell which one.

"Help's on the way," he whispered so quietly that no one could hear.

X moved into the room, his posture slightly bowed to keep the shadows falling over his face. The less anyone got too good a look at his features, the better. It took a great deal of effort not to look at the deflated passengers as he passed. He did notice that not all of the passengers were being held together as he had originally thought. That made his job a bit harder. Still, X was confident that so long as everyone kept their nerve they would all get out of this alive.

So far so good, X thought as he made his way through the dining car. They haven't noticed I'm not one of them.

X was only three steps from the door when the guard nearest him shouted at him. Naturally, it was the impatient one.

"Of course," X muttered as he slowed, but did not turn around to face the mountain man who had called to him.

The guard shouted again. X could only understand part of what was said from his broken dialect. It had something to do with X's shoes, but he was uncertain what.

X heard the mountain man's footsteps coming closer.

Then he realized what had happened. The guard must have noticed his footwear. The shoes of the mountain man the Agent had borrowed the clothes from had not fit him. He was still wearing the new hiking boots A.J. Martin had been sporting. Boots that did not match the mountain man disguise no matter how wet and dirty they had become.

X had underestimated the mountain men. The guard was far more perceptive than he had given him credit for. He would not make that mistake again.

Tensing, the Agent allowed the knife to fall from its sheath tied to his arm into his hand, handle first. The blade remained concealed within the sleeves of his coat.

"I'm talking to you!" the guard growled in fractured French as he grabbed X by the shoulder and spun him around to face him.

That's when Secret Agent X made his move.

X spun quickly.

Flipping the knife in his hand, X swung at the guard, slicing the air between them. As the Agent had anticipated, the startled guard took a step back and away from the slashing blade.

Off guard, the mountain man was no match for the martial arts kick X planted on his leg. Before he could react to the pain in his leg, X twisted, planting the side of his boot against the man's head. His enemy dropped like a stone, his head smacking the bolted-in-place dining table on his way down. "One down," X whispered as his focus shifted to his second target.

The guard with the axe was on the move.

With reflexes honed over the course of years, X dove toward the floor, scooped up the fallen mallet with his free hand, and hurled it at the approaching guard. The Agent's aim was steady and true. He heard a crunch of bone as the mallet found its mark, right between the mountain man's enraged eyes.

No longer a threat, the axe-wielding guard crumpled to the floor in a heap.

X barrel rolled away as the third mountain man's large staff smacked the floor where he had been just seconds earlier.

X abandoned the knife in mid roll as he grabbed the sword from the fallen guard's sheath and gave it a tug. The sword slid easily from the man's back and when Secret Agent X landed on his feet he held the sword at the ready.

"Easy now, Friar Tuck," X commented as he expertly twirled the sword easily in his hand. Sadly, he suspected the humor of the moment was lost on his shaggy opponent.

Like Robin of Sherwood's most trusted comrade, the mountain man was no slouch with the staff. X parried each thrust from the wooden staff with the sword. With each attack the mountain man's momentum increased.

X flicked his wrist, twirling the sword around for a better angle and pressed the advantage. Finally on the offensive, X managed to push his foe back a step. The mountain man was a skilled fighter. He made X work for every inch he took.

Maneuvering the Agent toward the tables, the man with the staff had him cornered. X bobbed as the staff passed by overhead, smacking the window and sending a spider's web of cracks along the glass pane.

"You know, we could probably call this a draw if you'd like to sit down and talk about this like gentlemen," X said as he kicked a chair at his opponent.

Dodging the wooden chair momentarily slowed the big man, just enough for X to plant his hands on the table and propel himself over it, kicking his foe while in mid-leap.

"Or not," X said with a mischievous grin as he landed smoothly, lifting his confiscated sword just in time to deflect another shot from the staff.

"I gotta hand it to you," X said as he dodged another blow from the staff. "You're good. Maybe the best I've ever faced under the circumstances."

The mountain man grunted.

"I'll take that as a compliment," X joked as he planted a foot in the man's midsection, doubling him over.

Another Judo kick sent the mountain man flying backward into the

"Easy now, Friar Tuck," X commented as he expertly twirled the sword easily in his hand.

bar. The few bottles and plates that had survived the train's untimely deceleration were knocked to the floor under the large man's impact. One of the passengers, the lady who had been knitting earlier, screamed as the man fell to the floor at her feet.

Before his foe could react, X kicked the staff away and brought the sword up under the mountain man's chin.

"Ah, ah, ah…" X said as he knelt near him, the sword still in place.

"What say you and I have a little chat," the Agent said.

An angry stare was his only answer.

"I know you're looking for something! What is it?"

"You know very well what we seek, outlander," the man finally said, his voice harsh, craggy.

X pulled back his hood so the mountain man could better see him, but not enough so the passengers could connect their savior to A.J. Martin. X had already put a plan together to explain the reporter's absence after this was over. X was always planning two steps ahead.

"If I truly knew, would we be having this pleasant little conversation?"

Silence.

"Yeah. Didn't think so," X said. "Spill it."

The mountain man's brow knit tightly as he struggled with the decision whether to trust the man with the blade of a sword at his throat.

"What are you looking for on this train?" X asked again.

"Retribution," the man finally admitted. "Someone on this train has killed us all."

The mountain man opened the door slowly.

X was a step behind, once again in possession of the knife he had taken off of the man who had fallen off the train with him. He still held the sword, but it was kept in reserve, the dull edge resting against the back of his arm and the hilt firmly in his palm. A simple flip of the wrist and the sword would be in the ready position. The weapons were well made and were perfectly acceptable for fighting in close quarters, but X would have preferred another kind of weapon altogether if he had his wish.

"What I wouldn't give for a couple trusty automatics at the moment," he whispered as they stepped into the first passenger car connected to the dining car. There were three passenger cars total.

"Let's just take it nice and easy," X said in his closest approximation of the man's broken French as they marched single file through the cramped passageway.

His captive grunted a soft reply.

"How many of you are there on this train?"

"Seven," he said after a polite jab with the point of the knife.

"Two down so only five more of you, huh?"

"Your incredible luck will not continue, outlander."

X smiled. "Oh, you'd be surprised at how much luck I've got. Keep moving."

X followed the mountain man down the corridor, the knife blade never more than inches from his captive's spine. Since their fight had ended, the man had made no attempt to flee or to shout a warning. Then again, X knew there was a very good possibility he was being walked right into an ambush.

Wouldn't be the first time, the Agent thought. *Guess I'll jump off that bridge when I come to it.*

"So, how exactly has someone on this train wronged you and your people?"

"You would not understand."

"Try me."

The mountain man stopped as if to consider it.

"Very well," he said, his voice falling to a hushed, almost reverent tone that told X that the savage act these mountain men displayed was just that, an act.

"I'm all ears," X said as he took a step back out of the man's reach.

"We are but a simple people, outlander. My people have lived in a small village out in the wilds of what we have heard called the Lost Valley. Such an ill-fitting name, I assure you. To us, it is simply home."

X nodded, but did not interrupt. It had taken a lot to get the man to start talking and he certainly did not want to do anything to stop him now.

"We value our seclusion but have been very hospitable to visitors when they approach our gates. Some of our people, usually the young and inquisitive ones, have even left us to travel out among the more 'civilized' people. Most return, thankful for the opportunity to have learned about the world, but even more thankful that they have a sanctuary from the dangers of your world.

"Several years ago there was a group of men who rode into our encampment on horseback. I was little more than a child at the time, not very old."

"How old are you now?" X asked.

"Older," the mountain man said as if he were ashamed of his age.

X smiled despite the seriousness of the situation. He assumed the man was, at best, in his early forties.

"These men came to us and we greeted them with the open hands of friendship."

"What happened?"

"They were not interested in our friendship," he said. "They were brutal. Many of my people were slaughtered that day. Including my father."

"And mine."

X had not heard the other mountain man enter the car behind him. He was now between them, boxed in. Trapped. X angled himself so his back was against the wall. The knife in one hand was pointed at his captive. A simple flip of the wrist brought the sword up and he had it pointed toward the new arrival.

"My father died that day as well. He was a hero who gave his life to save mine. Not all children were so fortunate."

"These people are not responsible," X said.

"No," the newcomer agreed. "No. They are not responsible for kidnapping the children or for the wholesale slaughter of my people so long ago. We are not savages, sir. We do know this."

"Then why?"

"Because someone did steal one of our most prized relics two nights ago. And we are certain that that person is aboard this train," the newcomer said.

"And when we find that person we will make him pay!"

"And what exactly is this relic?"

The mountain man stiffened, but made no move to sidestep the sword X had pointed at his throat. A simple lunge and he would be dead before his body hit the floor. Still, he did not reply.

"I asked you a question," X said, a hint of menace dripping off every word.

"It is difficult discussing this with an outlander."

"I suggest you make an exception," X said, emphasizing the sword pointed at the big man's neck. "Just this once."

The mountain man deflated.

"As you wish," he said. "Our people are governed by a matriarch: the village mother. The responsibility is passed down from one generation to another, from mother to daughter. It is a tradition we have upheld for many generations."

"Go on."

"During the raid those many years ago, the only daughter of our matriarch was taken from us. Attempts to conceive another daughter failed. We knew that she would be the last of the matriarchs unless she bore another child or, through some miracle, her daughter was returned to us."

"She's dead, isn't she?"

"Yes. Our matriarch crossed over several weeks past. For the first time in our long history we are without guidance. Old feuds have begun to rekindle. Without a matriarch to guide us, my people could very well tear themselves apart."

"I still don't see what that has to do with this train."

"The matriarch possessed an ornamental bracelet that signified her position of authority. Two days ago someone entered our village under the cover of darkness and stole the bracelet. We have been sent to retrieve it."

"Wait a minute," X said with a shake of his head. "All of this is over a bracelet?"

"I doubt it has much value in the outland world, but for my people it is an irreplaceable treasure that must be returned. It is the heart of our village and a vital piece of our history, which is very important to us."

"And you are certain this bracelet is on this train?"

"I am."

"So who has it?"

"I do not know."

"Then you see my problem."

"Yes, but you do not understand how important this item is to us."

"Then you'd better start explaining yourself," X said, annoyed.

"The bracelet protects us."

"Protects you?" X asked, not understanding. "Protects you from what?"

"It protects us…" the mountain man said, pausing before continuing. "From the creature."

"What creature?"

"If we do not get that bracelet back, the one who will kill us all."

The two men on guard outside the train paced back and forth.

They were apprehensive, but it was not the cold night air that chilled them. They were on guard in case the great beast reared its ugly head. So intent were they on making sure nothing sneaked up on them that they were not paying attention to what was already aboard the train.

Pierre Michon tightened his grip on the girl's arm. They were crouched beneath the train, hiding from the men walking back and forth, front to rear. There was no doubt that their lives were forfeit if they were discovered.

The girl, Anna, was trembling, as much from the cold as from sheer terror.

When the mountain men had boarded the train, the courier had stepped in front of the girl to keep her safe. There was no way of knowing what the savages might have done to the poor girl should they have gotten their hands on her.

He had acted on instinct, his soldier training kicking in automatically.

Moving with a speed he no longer thought he possessed thanks to his damnable wooden leg, Pierre dove for the light switch. As the dining car was plunged into darkness, he moved toward the rear door, pushing the girl ahead of him. The startled screams of the other passengers served to mask their escape through the rear door.

Once outside they dropped between the cars and scrambled forward through the snow toward the engine car. Without a winter coat or gloves, he knew they could not remain outside the warm confines of the train for very long. If he could not retake the engine car then he would have to find a safe spot to hide the girl.

The biggest problem would be finding a safe place with the mountain men all around.

"This way," he whispered.

Fighting back tears, the shivering Anna nodded and followed slowly.

By the time they reached the main car, both of them were exhausted and freezing. Pierre motioned for her to stay put while he made sure the coast was clear.

Her teeth were chattering so loudly that she assumed one of the men after them would hear, but she nodded that she would stay put. At least she thought she did. As much as she was shaking she wasn't completely sure.

The courier pulled himself up between the cars slowly, pausing halfway to make sure no one had spotted him. Once satisfied that they were alone, he stood and began to climb.

Suddenly, Pierre was snatched upward.

Anna gasped, choked back a scream.

Have they found us? she wondered.

Slowly, she crawled forward on hands and knees, no longer feeling the cold of the snow through her numbed fingers. Despite the fear that gripped her, she poked her head out from the safety of the train's underbelly. She looked up and her eyes widened in terror.

What she saw was beyond description.

It was a monster!

Anna gasped and the beast swiveled and looked down at her, blood and saliva dripping from its menacing razor-sharp teeth.

The beast dropped the bloody mess that had only moments before been Pierre Michon as it leaned down between the two train cars to get a better look at its next meal. Their eyes locked and Anna swore she could see its face curl up in a smile that scared her to the core.

The beast moved closer.

Anna screamed.

X heard the girl's scream.

Both he and the two mountain men started at the sound.

"What's happening?" X demanded.

The mountain man who had come up behind him turned and bolted from the car, back through the door leading to the landing between the first and second sleeper cars.

X was one step behind him.

The mountain man burst through the door and found himself face to face with a fur-covered monstrosity straight out of a nightmare.

The creature was massive. It crouched easily at five feet. Standing erect, it would have easily been well over seven feet tall. Once the creature's fur had been white, but the ravages of age and the harsh conditions of the Lost Valley had long since stained it varying shades of yellow and brown.

An apron of bright crimson blood ran from its mouth down the front of the creature's muscular body.

It snarled as it locked eyes with the mountain man.

The creature lunged at the startled man, but grabbed only air.

A split second before the creature attacked, Agent X had run out the door. Seeing the situation at hand, X's instincts took over and he tackled the frozen mountain man like a linebacker. Both men flew off the deck and crashed to the snowy ground below.

His prey out of reach, the creature bellowed in anger.

X and his new ally scrambled to their feet.

"What the hell is that thing?" X demanded.

"The creature!"

"Gee, you think?"

The creature leapt from its position straddling both cars.

"Move! Move!" X shouted as he spurred the mountain man to action. "Go! Go!"

The creature landed in the soft snow. Craning its massive head left then right, it sought out the easiest prey now that it had several to choose from.

The snarling smile returned when it saw the young, scrumptious morsel cowering beneath the train. The creature took a clawed step forward, then recoiled in pain.

X stood between the girl and the monster, the creature's blood dripping from the tip of his sword.

"Get the girl out of here!" he ordered.

"But..." the mountain man started.

"Go!"

The mountain man complied, grabbing Anna by the wrist and dragging her from her hiding place. So terrified was she that she went willingly, forgetting that she had originally been under the train hiding from the very man to whom she was now entrusting her life.

X stood his ground as the wild beast moved back and forth, its eyes never straying from its prey. The creature was cautious after X's first strike. It feinted left, then right, trying to catch the human off guard.

But Secret Agent X was too smart for that.

X lashed out at the creature, sending it a step backward.

"What's the matter, Big Foot?" X said. "You afraid of the pig sticker?"

A guttural roar escaped the wounded beast's throat as it leapt toward X.

The Agent stepped left and sliced at the monster as it sailed past. The beast's blood left a splatter trail along the railcar.

X twirled the sword around for a better grip and stepped forward to finish off the creature before it could kill again. Without warning, the beast lashed out, the backside of his massive clawed hand catching X in the midsection and tossing him back.

X landed with a grunt. Stunned, the sword fell from his grasp.

The creature was back on its feet. It advanced slowly on its enemy, saliva dripping from his long teeth.

X pushed himself back. He had to stay out of the monster's reach or he was done for.

"STOP!"

Amazingly, the creature followed the shouted command.

X turned to the owner of the voice. What he saw was unbelievable. Anna and the mountain man were standing near the train. The bracelet the mountain men were after was around her wrist. The girl had her hands held high, a soft glow pulsed from the metal object she wore.

"Heel!" she commanded and the creature softened.

Anna took a step forward. With each step she took, the beast retreated by the same distance.

It's afraid of the bracelet, X thought. *How is that possible?*

Anna stopped next to X. The creature stayed away as if allergic to the girl. The mountain man helped X to his feet.

"How exactly are you doing this?" the stunned Agent asked.

"Magic," the mountain man said.

"Would you care to elaborate?"

"No."

X took a step toward the girl. "Anna?" he said softly.

"Go home," she whispered, and the creature turned and ambled away as if it had lost all interest in them.

"Who are you?"

The girl turned to face him, tears streaking the grime on her face.

"She is the Matriarch," X heard the mountain man say from behind him.

X turned. "But I thought you said...."

The last thing he saw was the mountain man's fist just before impact.

X awoke in the baggage car.

Expecting an attack, he sat up quickly. However, there was no attack. The others in the frigid railcar sat there in stony silence. No one moved to stop X as he got to his feet.

"What's going on here?"

The big mountain man X had saved from the beast stood and took two steps toward the Agent. X tensed.

"Our business here is concluded," the mountain man said.

"Just like that?"

"We are releasing the train."

"And the girl?"

"She is coming with us."

"Oh, that's not going to happen."

"It's okay, Monsieur Martin," a familiar voice called from behind the mountain man.

"Anna?"

The young writer stepped from behind the large man even as he tried to position himself between her and X as if he were suddenly her protector.

"Are you okay?" she asked.

"I'll live," X said. "Are you all right?"

Anna smiled sheepishly, more like the girl he remembered meeting in the dining car as opposed to the girl who scared off monsters. "I am fine," she said.

"You don't have to go with them," X said.

The big mountain man bristled, but held his position.

"I'll protect you."

"It's okay, Monsieur Martin. I think I want to go with them."

"Why?" X asked. There was no way he was letting her out of his sight without a good explanation.

Sensing as much, Anna pulled her sleeve up, revealing a slightly tarnished golden bracelet. As jewelry it had no real aesthetic beauty. The only value was the gold from which it was made, but even that would not fetch much monetarily.

But X had seen the bauble in action. He knew its true power, though he was at a loss to explain exactly how it did what it did.

"You stole the bracelet from their village?"

"Kind of."

"I'm afraid you'll have to do better than that, kid."

"This bracelet belonged to my mother."

Realization dawned on X. "So you're...."

"Yes," she said. "As a child I was taken from the village by some very bad people. A kind man saved me from these bad people, but I was too young to explain where I came from, so he found me a home in his native country, America. I have lived there since. A few years ago, I discovered information on my home."

"So you came here looking to find a link to your past. I can understand that."

"Unfortunately, she arrived in time to find out her mother had died," the mountain man added.

"So you took the bracelet because...."

"Because it was all I have left of my past."

"And since your mother could use the weapon to stave off the creature, then so were you."

"Yes, but I did not know that until he told me."

"Are you sure you want to stay?"

"Yes. I want to learn more about... my people."

"I understand."

"Could you do me one favor?"

"Name it."

Anna handed X a folded envelope. "Please see that my adoptive family in America gets this. The address is on the front."

"I promise."

"Thank you. My men have cleared the track. As soon as we are away, the engineer will get you to France safely."

X watched as Anna and her protectors walked away into the stillness of the wintry night until the Lost Valley swallowed up any sign that they had been there. He was not sure what to make of the events of the day. He had seen many a strange sight in his day, but nothing that compared to that creature.

The train lurched as the engineer got them underway.

X tapped his pocket and smiled. The magnetic strip was right where he had left it.

His mission was over.

It was time to go home.

THE END

WHO IS SECRET AGENT X?

I must admit that when I signed on to write this Secret Agent X tale I really did not know a lot about the character. Oh, I was certainly aware of the character on the most basic of levels. I had heard the name and I remembered hearing that he was a master of disguise.

That was pretty much it.

Working on these pulp revival titles for Airship 27 has certainly expanded my reading list. That alone has made this job a joy. As I delved into the character of Secret Agent X, I started with the usual assortment of questions. Who is he? What does he do? Who's the girl? (What? Oh, come on! There's always a girl!) Who are his allies? Who are his enemies?

Like I said, the basics.

X, as he is affectionately called by those closest to him, is a warrior. I would even go so far as to say he was probably a war hero, but that could simply be conjecture on my part. Since no one, including Betty Dale (the aforementioned girl) actually knows X's true identity, there's really not a lot of the old trappings for the writer (that's me) to fall back on. You know, like little remembrances or things his Dad told him, or any of those little things we writers use to pad our word count (but all in the context of telling a good story, of course).

Something happened to X during "The War" that shaped his post WWI career as a crime fighter. He learned martial arts, jiu-jitsu and Judo primary among them. He learned how to fashion masks and to disguise himself. In fact, X was so good at it that he was dubbed "The Man of A Thousand Faces." He also has several permanent identities like A.J. Martin of the Associated Press. (What is it about super heroes and reporters?)

I found that part intriguing.

I was also drawn to the Secret Agent aspect. Upon reading some of the adventures of X (as I now affectionately refer to our hero) I noticed that the secret agent aspect of the character was not usually as focused upon as the crime fighter aspect. At least not in the way I envisioned a secret agent.

I grew up in an era of spy TV shows and movies. From James Bond to the Men (and Girl) from U.N.C.L.E., from the Six Million Dollar Man to Sydney Bristow, I'd observed many a secret agent. I had to find out what made our hero different from all the others.

So I put him in a classic secret agent setting.

And what could be more classic than an agent infiltrating an enemy installation, stealing valuable intel, and high-tailing it out of there before the bomb he planted wiped out the mysterious secret evil stronghold of his enemy? Nothing, of course. So I plucked our hero right in the middle of an assignment that would have done James Bond proud.

And I'm happy to report that Secret Agent X has no trouble playing in Bond's sandbox. Still, I wanted to focus more on his escape. That led X (and me) to the train.

Now, while I could go on and on (and on and on and on…) about the mystery of the infiltration skills of The Man of a Thousand Faces, his amazing brain, those brilliantly crafted gas pellets and gas guns, and especially the lovely Betty Dale and X's spectacular supporting cast (who, quite frankly, I hardly utilized this time around, but I'm sure the other writers in this volume will have more than made up for my lack of supporting characters), I won't.

There is so much rich history between the covers of the book you hold in your hand (and in volumes I , II and II of the Airship 27 series and numerous reprints of the original pulps) that shows you exactly who X is.

Secret Agent X is a bona fide pulp hero.

And the world could use a few more of those.

BOBBY NASH writes from his secret lair in the wilds of Bethlehem, Georgia. A multitasker, Bobby's certain that he does not suffer from ADD, but instead he... ooh, shiny.

When he finally manages to put fingers to the keyboard, Bobby writes novels (*Evil Ways, Fantastix*), comic books (*Fuzzy Bunnies From Hell, Demonslayer*), short prose (*A Fistful of Legends, Full Throttle Space Tales Vol. 2: Space Sirens, Green Hornet Case Files*), novellas (*Lance Star: Sky Ranger, Ravenwood: Stepson of Mystery*), graphic novels (*Yin Yang, I Am Googol: The Great Invasion*), and even a little pulp fiction (*Domino Lady,*

Secret Agent X) just for good measure. Despite what his brother says, Bobby is not addicted to buying DVD box sets and can quit anytime he wants to.

You can check out Bobby's work at www.bobbynash.com, www.lance-star.com, www.facebook.com/bobbyenash, and www.twitter.com/bobbynash, among other places across the web.

SECRET AGENT "X"

by Jarrod Courtemanche

Betty Dale was walking home one night after pulling a long shift in the newsroom. She was a reporter for one of the city's biggest newspapers and one of the only female news reporters around. She earned her way to the top through sheer determination, skill, and the fortunate good graces of men in charge who could see past the skirt and recognize true talent.

As she walked, Betty was overcome with that eerie feeling of being watched. She kept looking over her shoulder, expecting to find a pair of eyes burning holes in her back. There was nothing there. The streets were deserted. A siren wailed in the distance. Someone else in the city needed the boys in blue tonight.

Betty didn't stop looking though. She just couldn't shake it. She took this route, at this time, at least a hundred times and never felt as uneasy as she did now. It was a warm September night, but she wrapped her coat tight, shivering.

As she moved along, the fear grew worse. It was nearly a palpable thing, gnawing at her resolve. She began a rapid walk, heels clicking on the pavement. Her heart was thumping in her chest. She swallowed hard, choking down a cry. She began to run. Her apartment was only a block away.

Finally, she reached her door. Fumbling with her keys in haste, she let out a sob when she dropped them. Hands shaking she picked them up and forced a key into the lock.

"Please, please, please, work!" she cried. A single tear born of pure terror streaked down her cheek.

The lock clicked and she opened the door quickly, just a crack. It was enough to barely let in her slim figure before she slammed it shut and threw the bolt. She slumped down in front of the door and began to cry in earnest.

"What is wrong with me?" she asked.

She stood up and composed herself. She told herself there was nothing out there. No one was watching her. Nothing was after her. She hung her jacket on a peg and let her hair down. She had a long day ahead of her tomorrow and would need her beauty sleep. She made herself some tea to help calm her nerves. It was good going down. This would help. This was what she needed.

While undressing to get ready for bed, one last shiver ran down her spine. She glanced out the windows and saw a shadow steal across the full moon, the harvest moon. She drew the curtains tight and jumped into bed. She pulled the covers flush up to her neck and stared fearfully at the moving shadows on the ceiling.

Her eyes were still open come daybreak. She hadn't sleep a wink.

The next day, Betty walked numbly into work. She couldn't hide the bags under her eyes or the lag in her step. People at the office noticed the difference and made whispering comments behind her back. This only made her feel worse. She still didn't understand why she couldn't sleep. What drove her into such a panic?

At her desk, she had a story still in the typewriter from last night. She stared at the words on the paper and they morphed into unintelligible squiggly lines. She tried shaking her head and rubbing her eyes. It didn't work. She couldn't focus. She needed something to wake her up.

"Morning, sunshine!" the words came on cue. A.J. Martin, ace reporter for the Associated Press, showed up in front of her desk with a steaming cup of coffee. "You sure look like you could use this."

"Oh, thank you," she said, weakly. She wanted to stand up and hug him, but that wouldn't be appropriate in this setting. His very presence, though, gave her the strength she needed to carry on. Knowing who he was and what he did as Secret Agent X just made her feel safer. She took a sip of coffee and her nerves seemed to shrink back to a normal state.

"What happened to you," X asked. "I know it's not polite to comment on a woman's appearance, but I have to be honest. You look quite the worse for wear at the moment."

"I'm fine," she lied. "I just didn't sleep very well last night." She didn't want him worrying about her when he probably had enough on his plate.

X knew a lie when he heard one. He stepped closer and said quietly, "Seriously. Are you okay?"

"Yes," she said, looking around the office for eavesdroppers. "I'll talk to you later. It can wait."

"Okay then," X said loudly, acting more official. "I'll go see what your boss wants with me."

She waved bye when he left, then finished her coffee and started working on her deadline. She was able to focus now, but still looked up nervously every now and then, certain someone was watching her.

Surprisingly, the lack of sleep didn't impede her output. In true heroic fashion, Betty handed in all her assignments on time with nary a thank you from the boss. That was what she got for being the best. Expectations were high and anything less was considered insufficient.

She was working late again to get ahead on tomorrow's story, a piece about the shutting down of an underground drug manufacturer. Apparently, opium was making a comeback on the streets. Rumors of Secret Agent X discovering the plot to distribute the drug through the local high schools led to police arresting a well-known university professor. It seemed the professor was on some kind of revenge kick against all students because of an incident involving his wife and one student of his in particular. It was a long convoluted story that made for great press because new details would always come out later to continue enticing the public's right to know.

When she finished, she cleared her desk and stood up, arching her back to stretch it out after sitting for so long. She looked around the dark room. Shadows crept in from all angles, seemingly smothering light cast by her desk lamp and also streaking in from the windows.

She looked outside the office and saw Charlie, the night watchman, slumped in his chair, dozing. She gathered her things together and locked up the office door for the night. She lightly tapped Charlie on the shoulder until he sputtered awake.

"Hrrm, hrrm, a what? Who?" he muttered until he came to his senses. Charlie was an old Irishman who'd delivered newspapers all his life. Many people thought he had something illegal going on the side, but nobody could ever find anything. He was such a nice guy that no one wanted to look into it all that hard. Everyone needed a little extra dough from time to time. He was given the night watchman's job as a favor to all the reporters and news workers he met over the years.

"It's just me, Charlie," Betty said.

"Oh," he brightened and sat up straight. "Working late again, are we?"

"Yes," Betty couldn't help but smile. "I was wondering if you could do me a small favor tonight?"

"Oh, anything for you, Ms. Dale."

"Could you just walk me to the curb?" she asked.

"Why, certainly; Ms. Dale," he answered. "It would be my pleasure."

Betty didn't usually ask for the escort, but with the way she's been feeling lately, it couldn't hurt. The walk was slow due to Charlie's advanced age. This gave Betty time to think. She observed Charlie hobbling along weakly. *What could he do to protect me?* She thought. *More than likely, I would have to protect him from any assailant. I'm actually more vulnerable right now than if I would have made the trip downstairs myself.* She began to regret asking Charlie to do this. The thought continued to nag at her until she finally couldn't contain herself.

"Charlie," she said. "That's far enough. I can take it from here."

"Oh," Charlie was crestfallen. "Okay, Ms. Dale. As you like."

Betty walked on at a quickened pace. She exited the building then stopped and leaned up against the wall. Her pulse was rapid. Calm down, she thought. Why did she brush Charlie off like that? He was the sweetest man. Now she was all alone with the dark night between her and a decent night's sleep. How she wished Secret Agent X was here.

She made her way along the dark street, hugging the wall and constantly looking out for danger. She didn't make it one block before she started shaking in fear, her knees knocking together and her teeth chattering.

"Who are you?" she whispered. She didn't expect an answer. She didn't really believe there was anyone around. She just needed to ask.

The buildings seemed to close in on her as she continued. They were menacing, evil, leering things with windows for eyes that lacked a soul and doors for mouths that could swallow you whole. She edged out into the street to get away from them.

Another block from home and a gust of wind tore threw her, blowing the pins right out of her hair. She had to hold onto her coat for dear life to keep it from being ripped off her body. She ran and took shelter in the alley beneath her apartment building.

At the end of the alley the wind died down to be replaced by pure darkness. The light of the street lamps unnaturally failed to reach past the alley's yawning opening. Blind, Betty began to crawl on hands and knees. She only went a few feet before her hand slipped on something viscous and slimy.

"No," she whimpered. She felt lost. She didn't know which way was out. She began shaking uncontrollably. She curled up into a ball and cried.

Somewhere out of the darkness a low, whispering, evil laugh called out, taunting.

Betty screamed.

"Betty!" yelled Secret Agent X, currently disguised as ace reporter A.J. Martin. He was shaking her gently but fervently, trying to get her attention.

"Betty!" he yelled closer to her ear. Finally, she seemed to recognize his voice and she stopped screaming. Then she darted into his arms and held

She curled up into a ball and cried.

on tight, shaking and afraid to let go.

"Martin," she whimpered. "Martin, help me. Please don't let him get me. Please help me."

"Shush, now," he said. "It'll be all right. Everything will be all right."

Germany, three years ago:

Surrounded by beakers, pipettes, mini-rectifiers, and flasks, Doctor Faustus Von Furchtohne worked at a feverish pace. He was trying to satisfy two masters. The German politicians who set him up here demanded a new type of biological weapon to fight their enemies. They were fascists, and their rise to power would try to unite science with the military, making them a force to be reckoned with across the globe. His only family, his sister Agna, was born deaf. He made it his purpose in life to find a cure for her. While he couldn't care less for the military machine, he couldn't find her cure without it.

To these politicians he made promises that would be impossible to keep. He worked on their time for his sister, using electricity to spark sound into a viable curative wave that would repair broken cellular structure in the eardrum. He had developed a low power battery that could be inserted into a hand-held device for precise work on emitting sound waves in a tightly confined area. The device resembled a gun, to fool his superiors into thinking he was creating a weapon. He called it "Soundbreaker."

Just as he was completing a titration on a sulfosalicylic acidic solution, the door to his lab burst open. The sound of the door slamming against the wall startled him so much he dropped the Erlenmeyer flask onto the floor, shattering it and spraying acid over his shoes. There went hours worth of work down the drain and a pair of shoes that wouldn't last the month without falling apart.

Two men entered, one in a starched military uniform and carrying a rifle, the other in a smart business suit. The soldier stood to one side, ready and poised for trouble. The other man walked straight up to Faustus, one eyebrow raised as a seemingly permanent symbol of impatience.

"Well, Herr Doctor," he began. "Do you have a formula yet?"

"It's almost ready, Herr Lothar." Faustus lied. "I just need a few more days."

"Not good enough!" Lothar yelled. "I've waited too long, Doctor. I need to report a result now! Show me what you have so far."

"But I don't know if it's even going to work," explained Faustus, sweat forming on his brow. "The formula is unstable and could produce unwanted results."

"It matters not," the man sneered. He had a crooked nose that twitched with his words. He turned to the soldier. "Bring in the volunteer."

The soldier saluted in the Nazi tradition and hurried out of the room. Seconds later he came back in dragging with him an emaciated prisoner, cuffed and chained at the ankles and wrists. They threw him down into a chair. The man was unable to resist, helpless as a babe.

"What's this?" cried Faustus. "This is a volunteer?"

"Of course he is," Lothar crowed. "Do you think he wants to continue his existence like this?"

"No," Faustus said. "I won't do it."

Lothar just smiled, "Bring in our other guest."

The soldier left momentarily and quickly returned with a wide-eyed Agna in tow.

Faustus screamed in frustration.

Agna, wearing naught but her nightclothes, stared in mute shock at her surroundings. Her gaze fell on Faustus, her confusion wrenching at his heart.

"Now!" Lothar pointed at the volunteer. "Either test your formula on the subject, or your dear sister will be joining him in the volunteer cells."

"No," Faustus whispered. His sister. So innocent and unaware. He couldn't contain his emotions any longer. Tears poured down his cheeks in rivulets. "You don't know what you're asking."

Lothar stomped over to Agna and grabbed a fist full of hair. "Do it now! Or I'll snap her neck!"

Faustus gathered himself together. "Fine." He adjusted the settings on his device, Soundbreaker. He inserted the low-powered battery into the handle. He aimed carefully at the volunteer's right ear. He pulled the trigger.

Chaos erupted.

First, the volunteer gave such an ear-piercing scream that it almost popped his eardrums. The man made a mad thrust at the soldier. Hobbled by the manacles, he merely fell into him. The soldier panicked as well, firing his gun wildly, bullets ripping through the air, glass shattering. Electricity crackled as bullets tore through components and consoles. The volunteer was a ragged and bloody mess, torn nearly in half by the volley of gunfire. The soldier finally dropped the gun and began screaming to get the man off of him. Lothar stood in shock, unable to move through a self-induced haze of paralysis. Agna, oblivious to the sounds around her, curled up on the floor in a fetal position, trying to block the world away.

Faustus looked around at the effect his device had. He saw it less as chaos and more of a cacophonous symphony, an artful opera of scream and fear personified. For some reason he was unaffected by his own device. For reasons he didn't yet understand, this pleased him. The soldier finally stopped shooting to grab at his own ears and run straight at a window. He jumped right through the stained glass, shattering the hard work of artisans many years gone. The wooden shutters couldn't contain his momentum and he plunged three stories to his death.

Faustus next looked at Lothar. He was stilled, paralyzed with fear, his mouth working silent words of horror. Righteous anger surging through his veins, Faustus walked up to Lothar and stared him in the eye. Lothar whimpered.

"You fool," Faustus spat. "I told you it wasn't ready. But do you listen? No! Pig-headed bureaucrat! Now, pay for your idiocy!"

Faustus placed the device next to Lothar's head and activated it once again. Lothar screamed and began tearing at his own face, trying to scrape away the terror. He fell to the ground and dragged himself on his knees to the door all the while doing irreparable harm to his own skull. Finally, he lay down and died, literally tearing himself apart.

His revenge complete, Faustus turned his attention to Agna. She was still in the same fetal position on the floor.

"Agna," he walked over to her. "Agna, come. Get up." He shook her gently. "Agna?" There was no response. He turned her over and looked with horror upon the blood on the floor. She had been struck by a stray bullet. She gave him one last look of confused innocence and beauty before she gave her last breath and died in his arms.

"Agna!"

"What's the matter with her, doc?" Secret Agent X, as A.J. Martin, asked the old man examining Betty Dale.

"Well," said the old man with the bushy eyebrows and horn-rimmed glasses. "Nothing, physically. But this poor girl has been through some severe psychological trauma. I am talking about classic Freudian diagnosis. Far beyond my expertise, I'm afraid. She should see a psychiatrist." The doctor's aged voice shook with the effort of speaking.

"I am sitting right here, you realize," Betty huffed. "And I am not just some poor girl."

"Pardon me, dear," the doctor patronized, patting her hand gently like a doting father.

Betty just rolled her eyes and shook her head.

"Thanks, doc." X escorted the old man out of the room and closed the door behind him.

"Where did you find him?" Betty asked, exasperated.

X smiled. "He's an old friend from the war. He may be antiquated, but he knows his stuff."

Betty grabbed her coat and put it on.

"Where do you think you're going?" X asked.

"You heard the good doctor," she quipped. "I'm fine. I'm going home."

"Betty wait," X pleaded, touching her elbow lightly. Betty retreated almost instinctively from the contact. "Please tell me what happened out there?"

Betty stopped for an instant, staring into space, searching for some kind of explanation that would make sense. "I don't know," she said slowly. "I've never felt anything like that. After all the things I have experienced; all the adventures I've been through with you and investigating things on my own, I thought I was immune to being scared. I thought I could handle anything. Now it seems I'm just a scared little girl, screaming at shadows."

"I don't believe that for a second," X said. "You are one of the bravest people I've ever met, and I've met a lot."

Betty waved him off. "You're just trying to make me feel better."

"No," X said, thoughtfully. "I'm not. I have a hard time believing that the woman who has helped me through dozens of dangerous missions is suddenly afraid of the dark, so much so that it incapacitates her. No. There is something else happening here and I plan on finding out what." He finished more forcefully, offering his arm. "Now let me walk you home."

"Fine," Betty sighed. "But I think you have more important things to do."

"Let me be the judge of that," X finished as they walked out the door.

Later that night, as X stood guard outside the door of her apartment, Betty tossed the blankets aside in a fevered dream. Sweat drenched her nightclothes. She thrashed against some unknown vision. "No. No, no, please," she pleaded silently. Her eyes popped open suddenly, staring into the ruddy glow of her lamp. "Fifth time," she whispered. "Fifth time tonight. How much longer can I go on like this?"

Out in the hallway, Secret Agent X paced back and forth. He needed to check in with his operative, Harvey Bates at the Colonial Research Foundation. Secretly a cover for his operations, the Foundation was where Harvey gathered information that he correlated into useful clues to help Secret Agent X fight saboteurs, gangsters and other threats to his nation's security. Harvey's information helped X figure where best to fight these threats, and what priority each one took. X looked at his watch. Half past midnight. He'd been here five hours and not a peep.

Suddenly, he heard a blood-curdling scream. His first thought was that it couldn't be Betty. He couldn't imagine such a sound coming out of her delicate throat. There must be someone else, or something else. He burst through the door of her apartment, expecting to tackle some horrific half-beast. Instead, he saw Betty scream again, blooded nails clawing at the wall, trying to escape some unknown nightmare. The sound cut through his spine, an involuntary twisting of vertebrae causing a phantom pain that wretched his nerves.

He made his way to the window. Looking across to the other building, he saw a figure pointing something right at him. He ducked down quickly, thinking it might be a gun, but no shot was fired. When he peered over the sill again, the figure was gone. Looking back at Betty he saw that she had stopped clawing the wall. She was now huddled in a quivering heap, hugging her knees to her chest and sobbing uncontrollably.

X wanted to try to track down the strange figure, but he couldn't leave Betty in such a sorry state. He went over to her and reached out, whispering soothing words.

"No!" she cringed at his touch, trying to get away from him as though he was the assailant of her mind. She tried digging her already worn and bleeding nails into the wall, as if to climb. Falling to the floor, she then tried scrambling under the bed. X quickly backed up and Betty then stayed curled in her fetal ball, half hidden by the scrambled bed sheets.

This was no good, X thought. Betty needed help and he had to take her to it. She seemed to be reduced to sheer animal fight-or-flight instincts. In the past, X had encountered his share of wild animals that displayed the same characteristics that Betty now did. He would deal with them by using a special hypnosis technique he had learned while traveling the orient. It was a talent that normally didn't work on a reasoning, functional human. Sometimes the technique involved an intricately designed whistle he kept on his person at all times, and sometimes it involved his own impressive vocal mimicry involving a range of clicks, whistles, grunts, and coos.

He began to emit a series of soothing sounds, twitching slightly in rhythm with his incidental music. He tried various reverberations until he discovered one that seemed to have an effect. Betty stopped at the sound, the shaking in her limbs subsiding and the whites of her eyes yielding to their normal baby blue. She crawled into his arms, exhausted from her ordeal, and passed out from the strain. X lifted her gently in his powerful arms and strode out of the room.

Later, Secret Agent X stood outside of a room in the psychiatric wing of the hospital. He clenched his fists in rage as he watched orderlies restrain Betty as she went through another bout of irrational screaming. He knew that this fear she was experiencing wasn't natural. He stood and watched, and studied. He couldn't let his emotions get the better of him.

"I'll find the one who did this to you, Betty," he said out loud. "I'll find him and I will make him pay dearly." Exhibiting an extreme level of self control, X strode calmly out of the hospital to begin his hunt.

New York, one year ago:

In a laboratory at Brooklyn College, Professor Faustus Von Furchtohne was putting the finishing touches on a new formula he had devised for his latest version of Soundbreaker. He had made quite a few adjustments over the years. He had complete control of the direction and intensity of the wave emissions. He now felt he could fine tune the emissions to account for size, sex, and obstacles. Every factor caused a different effect. Was the subject wearing a hat? Were they behind a window? How thick was the pane? On and on the list of variables went.

The College was only eight years old, still a baby in this city. It sat in a forty acre field in the Flatbush section of Brooklyn and was the first public co-educational liberal arts college of its kind. The College was a place for the underprivileged, a place for immigrants, working peoples, and other such financially strapped members of society. Faustus believed the whole notion to be mildly ridiculous, but it was a means to an end. It was a low-profile job that gave him the time to conduct his own experiments. He never gave up trying to find the proper formula to repair the chronically deaf.

He came to America broken in both mind and body. After the incident that killed his little sister, his Agna, he stowed away on a steamboat that dropped him off at Ellis Island. The trip was excruciating. He survived by catching rats and cooking them on one of the hot engine pipes. The insides were always raw and foul, but he did what he could to survive.

Seeing that glorious Lady with her torch held high and the promise of knowledge and justice in her book led Faustus to an epiphany. He must balance the scales. Agna was taken away from him for no good reason other than the war-mongering greed of governments. So he would seek to balance those scales by tearing down every government he could.

So he continued to perfect his Soundbreaker, making it the ultimate weapon against everything he thought unjust.

Just then, the door burst open.

"Fichtone!" the speaker was a short balding man with the voice of a screeching crane. The sound cut through Faustus as if someone scraped his vertebrae with a boning knife. The fact that this man was his boss coupled with the horrible mispronunciation of his name germinated an especially vile hatred within his breast.

"Yes," Faustus replied with gritted teeth. "How can I help you, Dean Withers?"

"You missed the laying of the foundation for the new gymnasium today!" the Dean yelled. "The President himself was there! How could you be so absent-minded?"

Faustus turned his back on the man and continued tweaking Soundbreaker. "I suppose it just wasn't that important to me."

"What!" the Dean screeched. "What kind of dull-headed nitwit thinks a visit by the President of the United States isn't important!"

Faustus continued ignoring him.

"Listen to me, you idiot!" the Dean went up to the counter and smacked Soundbreaker away. The instrument made a horrible clatter as it flew across the floor.

"No!" Faustus cried. He rushed over to his contraption, lifting it gently off the floor. It can't be broken. It just can't!

"What are you doing coddling that thing like it matters?" the Dean scoffed. "You should be ashamed of yourself. Oh, and if you miss another important event like this again, you'll be fired!"

Faustus rose slowly, rage in his eyes. He stepped up slowly to the Dean, Soundbreaker firm in his hand.

"Now what are you doing here, Fichtone?" the Dean trembled slightly.

"You will never say my name again," Faustus whispered. "Nor will anyone else. From now on, I will be known as Doctor Fear!" He put Soundbreaker up against the Dean's sweaty temple and pulled the trigger. The Dean let out a blood-curdling screech then dropped to the floor, dead.

Doctor Fear fled into the night, laughing maniacally all the way.

Detective Burks was on the trail again. He'd been scouring the subway, looking for traces of Secret Agent X. He'd heard reports of a strange man haunting the dark tunnels beneath the city's streets and he knew it had to be X. The villain probably had a secret hideout down here and he was determined to find it.

He had gone through tunnel after tunnel, from Bedford Park to Central Park West to Queens Plaza, and still nothing. He had decided to make his way down to Brooklyn next when he spotted a dark figure in the distance. He gave chase right away hoping his quarry was in site. At the very least, he could arrest someone for vagrancy.

As he approached the area where he saw the dark figure, he suddenly felt as if he was being watched. He looked around nervously, trying to spot his unknown voyeur. Not seeing anyone, he continued on his path, more careful than ever. The tunnel seemed to be growing darker, the shadows closing in on him. He started sweating on his brow. A rat squealed as he stepped on its tail. He jumped in the air, startled by the creature. *What's the matter with me,* he thought. *I'm jumping at nonsense.*

A sudden clang brought him up short. There, in that side tunnel, Secret Agent X must have gone upside. Burks ran down the tunnel. It was wet, dampness oozing in through cracks in the stone. He saw a shaft of light illuminating a steel rung ladder going to the surface. He sprinted towards the ladder. Half way there, his foot lost purchase on the slick stones and he tumbled sideways, slamming his elbow into the wall and falling hard on his back.

Evil laughter echoed from above.

"New York's finest doesn't stand a chance against me!" the voice taunted.

"I know that's you, X!" Burks screamed. His clothing was soaked in the putrid water of the subway system. He tried to get up and slipped again, falling face first this time. A palpable fear took hold of him now. *Agent X has me trapped! He can finish me off anytime! He's just toying with me!*

Burks crawled forward an inch at a time, the effort straining his taxed muscles, draining his will. Sounds of hushed whispering permeated the area, coming from all directions. *Agent X's minions! His countless minions come to finish me off!*

A final evil laugh was cut off by the booming sound of a manhole cover sealing the exit. The tunnel was enveloped in darkness. Burks was trembling uncontrollably. The darkness was disorienting. He lost his sense of direction. He crawled along in the muck, feeling the walls for any kind of object that would mark his place. Agent X did this! Agent X left him down here to die. He wouldn't get away with it!

Burks screamed his defiance to all the dark denizens of his new Abyss. "Help! Get me out of here!"

Later, Subway workers discovered Burks just two feet from the ladder rung. He was shivering uncontrollably, his jaw clenched in an apoplectic rage. The men couldn't get him to tell them what happened. He just kept mumbling over and over again, "Secret Agent X. Must arrest Secret Agent X. He's after me. He's out to get me. He's out to destroy the world. Must stop Secret Agent X. Secret Agent X."

Secret Agent X was closer than Detective Burks would have been comfortable with. He was standing outside another room in the psychiatric wing of the hospital. Disguised as Police Captain Rosenburg, he stared through a small door window at the twisting form of Burks. Burks, a top-rate detective, was raving madly about how Secret Agent X put him in here. It made no sense to X, who, despite being the subject of Burks' ire, had the utmost respect for his abilities. The man was responsible for bringing to justice many criminals.

A young doctor approached. He had high cheekbones and an aquiline nose with Mediterranean olive skin.

"The symptoms are the same as Miss Dale's, Captain," he stated.

"Thank you, doctor," X said. It was time to step up the hunt for this mysterious assailant who seemed to be inflicting a strange psychosis on normally rational people.

X made his way outside to his black, non-descript sedan parked on the street. Inside he made a call to Harvey Bates. He needed some disseminated information that only Harvey could dig up through his network.

"Agent X to base," X intoned over the two-way radio. "Agent X to base. Come in, over."

"Base here," came Harvey's deep baritone over the speaker. "Go ahead."

"I need any information you can give me on all the leading experts in the area of sound-based technology." X wasted no time with further explanation.

"Got it, Boss," Harvey replied. "Over and out."

It wouldn't be a long wait for X to get his information. The network was very fast and quite reliable. The people reporting the information only knew they were telling a trusted confidant what they had. That confidant in return was telling someone else they knew very well who was directly associated with one of X's many guises.

In the meantime, Secret Agent X needed to figure out who this villain's next target would be.

Across the street from the hospital, on a rickety fire escape, Doctor Fear held a small device to his ear. He listened intently to the device, as if trying to listen to a conversation through the door to another room. Finally, when the black sedan sped into the night, Doctor Fear let the device down and smiled grimly.

"So," he said. "This Agent X thinks he can track me down." A wicked chuckle escaped his throat. "I'll show him what I think of that."

After visiting several well known professors, Secret Agent X was beginning to get disgruntled with his efforts. Every expert in the field that he talked to said it was impossible for a ranged weapon to have the kind of effects on the human mind that X had described. X assured them all that such a thing existed, but they all pleaded ignorance or thought X was some kind of crackpot.

The crackle of static issuing from the radio receiver interrupted X's thoughts.

"Base to X! Base to X!" Harvey's voice was unusually rushed. "Come in Boss!"

"What is it?" X said calmly.

"You better get back to the hospital right away. Someone left a note for you."

"Got it. X out." X spun his black sedan around the next bend, screeching tires wailing out his concern. He flew by pedestrians and other vehicles alike, causing onlookers to voice their concerns to the passing wind.

When he arrived at the hospital he parked across the street, studying the entrance closely. Fortune was on his side when he recognized the young doctor he had spoken to while in disguise as the police captain. The doctor was leaving the hospital and walking his way. X stepped out of his car, placing a worn, brown fedora over his head and down across his eyes. He pulled the collar of his coat up high. When the doctor came closer he pulled out a cigarette.

"Got a light, *mon ami?*" he asked the doctor in a smooth, silky French accent.

"Certainly," said the doctor. He displayed an air of professional courtesy that belied his youthful appearance.

Leaning in with a match, the doctor was completely unprepared for the puff of smoke that X blew out of the other end of the cigarette. The Doctor's surprise was short-lived as he choked and then collapsed against the car in a faint.

X caught the man gently and dragged him into the vehicle. He quickly worked to remove the doctor's clothing and his own. Next he applied his specially designed facial putty to his own features. He worked the putty expertly, pulling and twisting the mixture to mimic the exaggerated features of the doctor. Finally, a high gloss make-up was spread over the features to bring out the same olive sheen. Fortunately, he didn't have to adjust his hair too much. They had similar hairstyles and color. The doctor would be passed out a few hours giving X plenty of time to investigate the mysterious note. Donning the white smock as a final touch, he headed into the hospital.

Coming to Betty's quarters, X grabbed her chart off the door, looking busy so nobody would bother him. He noticed on the chart that they got her to take pills instead of giving her shots directly. That was a good sign. The Doctor's jacket he was wearing had a set of keys in them. Being familiar with all kinds of locks, X studied the key hole for this particular door and matched up the grooves with a singular key on a ring of multiple keys in the set with hardly a glance. He entered Betty's room and quickly closed the door.

Betty was sitting cross-legged on her bed. She seemed to be meditating except for the fact that sweat ran down her face and she was tense rather than relaxed. X approached cautiously.

"Betty," he whispered.

No response. He walked around in front of her. Her eyes were clinched shut.

"Betty," he offered. "It's me."

"Leave me alone," she said between clenched teeth.

"Oh, Betty," he sighed. "I want to help. I'm working on tracking down the maniac who did this to you."

Suddenly, she let out a piercing scream and grabbed him by the collar. "Don't you understand? I'm fighting it! Like you taught me! But I can't concentrate with you here!"

"The pills, do they help?" he asked.

"No!" she shrieked. "I will beat this! By myself!"

Suddenly, the door opened and an orderly stormed in. X quickly disengaged himself from Betty's grasp.

"Is everything all right in here, Doctor?" he asked.

"Yes," X immediately recovered. "I have it all under control."

"Okay," the orderly said, confused. "I thought you had already left, Doctor."

"I just had to check one more thing," X said. "By the way, was there a note left for me here?"

"I don't know if it was for you or not. There was an envelope on the door that said, 'do not open until X-mas,' and the X was in red ink. We called the police and they're on the way here."

"Give it to me," X commanded. "The X is a code from an old colleague of mine."

"Oh, let me get it." The orderly left.

X looked back at Betty and she was right back in her sitting position, tense and concentrating.

"I'll get him, Betty," he whispered as he left. "I swear it."

The orderly met him in the hallway with the wax-sealed envelope.

"Are you sure about this, Doctor?" he asked. "It seemed real suspicious just sitting up there like that."

"Yes," X said. "Call the police and tell them it was a false alarm."

When the orderly left, X stared at the envelope a minute, wondering how this turn of events came about. Something didn't fit. The orderly was too helpful. He gave in too easily. There wasn't enough confusion.

X took off down the hallway, racing in the direction the orderly went. He had to catch him! He raced to the stairs and opened the exit doorway. Looking down the stairwell, he saw the basement door slam shut. He swung over the third floor railing and leapt to the next level, landing and jumping in an incredible display of acrobatics that would put an Olympic gymnast to shame.

When he arrived at the bottom and flung open the door, his eyesight went black at the sudden transition from well-lit hospital to darkened alley. After his eyes adjusted, he looked for signs of passage.

There! A piece of trash had a footprint imbedded into it on the right side of the alley opening. X ran out of the alley into the busy street. Pedestrians of all kinds walked to and fro, about their daily business. Finding a lone man in the crowd would be nearly impossible for anyone else, but X had learned over the years to look for those telltale signs of someone trying to escape. He spotted the slight shrug and glance over the shoulder of his target, still within running distance. X darted across the street, leaping over car bumpers and causing horns to go off.

The orderly, now dressed in a different coat, saw the commotion and took off in a run. Several people were pushed aside in his frantic flight, falling into a news vendor and spraying newspapers in a high, wide arc. X dashed through the pulpy storm, ripping headlines out of his sight while keeping up the full speed chase.

As he passed a subway terminal, the orderly cut down an alley. X noted the alley and stopped. He backtracked to the terminal and raced down the stairs. Flying over railings, ignoring the startled looks of passengers and employees, X raced into a maintenance tunnel. He slipped between piping and stone, weaving his way seamlessly through the twisting passage as if he had worked here for years. Which in a way, he has. No one knew this city the way X did. He studied every nook and hole and knew it as a blind man knew his own home.

X climbed up a ladder and exited a trap door with an awning cover. Careful not to make any noise, he scoped out his surroundings. If his guess was right, he should be ahead of his prey. Taking cover, he waited.

Soon enough he heard the quick patter of running feet. The orderly approached, oblivious to his presence. He had slowed down to look behind him, wary, yet hopeful he lost his pursuer. His back turned, he had no clue what fate awaited him.

X snuck up behind him and quickly placed the orderly in a strong-arm hold, dragging him to the ground and shoving his knee in his back. The man didn't even have time to scream as the wind was stolen from his lungs by the sudden pressure on his chest and back.

X leaned close to his ear, breathing heavy into the cavity. He spoke in a low, growling voice. "Who hired you?"

The orderly twitched at the question. The proximity of X's voice to his eardrum seemed to cause undue stress and irritation to the man. He gasped in pain.

"I don't know!" he exclaimed. "Some older man with a strange accent. European maybe!"

X flipped him over, maintaining the hold on his arm. "Give me something to work with, scum! I have no aversion to breaking your arm!"

"Y-y-y-you're not Doctor Calla!" the orderly was truly frightened. His eyes white.

"That's correct," X said. "So you'd better come clean. I work for the U.S. government and the man who hired you could be a German spy. Anything you can tell me would benefit."

"Look," the orderly whimpered. "He just said to give it to the first man who asked about a letter while visiting Ms. Dale. I asked him who he was and he said he was a professional peer of Doctor Calla's from Brooklyn College."

"Why did you run?"

"He told me to!" the orderly cried. "He said I wouldn't want to be around when you got the bad news."

The letter! "Right, get out of here." X let the man go. He reached in his coat and opened the letter with the red X on it. It read:

Herr X,

I am on to you, sir. I hear everything you do. I hear every voice in this city. It is too bad about your friend, Ms. Dale. Such a shame for such a beautiful woman to be in such a state. Regardless, unless you can secure me forty million dollars, my next victim will be someone in a much more prominent position in this city. Perhaps the deputy mayor? Or maybe the mayor himself. No? You've seen what I can do. Do not make yourself think you can stop me. I assure you my wrath will be significant. You have two days. I will contact you again with details.

Doctor Fear

X crumpled the letter in his hand.

Betty Dale was not actually angry at Secret Agent X. She was quite pleased at the results of his visit earlier. The anger and concentration he forced her to display helped her to focus her thoughts. It made her confront her fears by naming them. One of her greatest fears was disappointing the man she loved. She knew by his visit that he needed her help. He wouldn't ever admit such a thing, not with her in this condition, but she knew he needed her.

After he left, she renewed her focus, concentrating all her efforts on purging her mind of the fears that had run rampant the past two days. She remembered the unnatural darkness. She remembered the evil laugh in the night and the other sounds that came out of it. She focused on the fact that someone, someone evil and bitter, set up that scenario, used it to frighten her. They used it as a test. She was sure of that. She was an experiment, a lab rat. Focusing on the scientific aspect of it helped her deal with her fears. Once she took out the superstition, once she understood the man-made conditions of her plight, she knew she could fight back. She knew she was capable of conquering fear.

The bolt on the door to her room opened and the night nurse entered. Dressed in traditional white, she carried with her a tray of implements for grooming.

"Hello, dear," she said in a motherly voice. "Let's just fix you up a bit, shall we?" The hospital made it a policy to have their patients looking somewhat presentable for visiting dignitaries. This was to ensure that those who provided funding knew that patients were being taken care of.

"May I brush your hair?" the nurse asked.

"Can I do it?" Betty asked back. "Please," she pleaded, trying to look pained.

"Well now, dear, you know I'm not supposed to let you have these things," the nurse admonished.

"I'll be good," Betty said. "I promise. I need this. I need my dignity back. You can hold the mirror," she finished hopefully.

Her pleading worked. The nurse, sympathy welling up in her eyes, gave Betty the hair brush and held a small mirror for her to use. Staring at her reflection, Betty considered what a mess she had become. Her hair was wild and tangled and there were bags under her eyes. She tore through the tangles on her head like weeds in a garden. After that, she asked if she could have some make-up. The nurse agreed and helped her apply it. During the makeover session, Betty secreted a pair of tweezers under her arm. Acting casual, she held her arm tight against her body to keep the tweezers hidden.

When the nurse left, Betty quickly dressed herself. She knew the staff would not allow her to leave. She straightened her newly combed hair, pulling it back into a tight bun and using a string out of the mattress to secure it. Fortunately, the clothing she wore when admitted was one of her best professional outfits. They even had them cleaned for her during her stay.

The lock on the door would be another problem. It wasn't a particularly secure lock, being a simple bolt thrown through a housing, but she lacked proper tools. She used the tweezers stolen earlier to slip through the crack in the door. Gently probing the bolt, she was barely able to squeeze the tip of the implement onto the shaft. Ever so slowly, she turned the shaft so that the prongs were in the correct position to slide the bolt over. After what seemed liked hours, she was able to slide the bolt over micro inch by micro inch. The movement was so subtle that anyone walking by wouldn't notice.

Betty listened at the door. When she was sure of no presence out in the hallway, she took a moment to compose herself. She wanted to act natural, confident, as if she owned the place. Secret Agent X once taught her that the best way to move around in any building was to act as though you belonged there. It was what he liked to call 'hiding in plain sight.'

She opened the door and stepped out into the hallway. A late night aura of calm hung over the hospital, that time when the hustle and bustle of the day blissfully sank into a relieved rest. Betty made her way down the abandoned hall, shoes clicking purposefully in a cadenced march. She avoided the main nurse's station and went around to the back staircase. When she got to the second floor, she went straight to the foyer where people were still performing various tasks. A sudden fear grasped her chest, choking off her air flow. She closed her eyes and gripped the railing. The panic was back. The walls were closing in. Everyone here was out to get her.

"Miss, are you okay?" a young voice said.

The sound was a light in the dark. Betty focused on it, opened her eyes and looked down at a child. Innocent eyes pulled her into their depths, breaking through the fear. She knelt down and looked at the child on his level. Wide open fearlessness looked back at her. How could she, an intelligent, capable adult, be struck with paralyzing fear, when confronted with such open trust? This child had not yet learned what fear is. Betty took strength from that. If fear can be learned, then it can be unlearned.

"Thank you," she whispered to him. "I'm just fine."

Betty straightened up and walked right out the front door of the

"Miss, are you okay?" a young voice said.

hospital. Not a single person stopped to question her. Not a single person would have ever thought she was a patient in the psychiatric ward. She had a job to do.

Two days! X couldn't give into this madman. It wasn't the money. X was sure his benefactors could easily gather the necessary funds. Secret Agent X could not let this self-styled Doctor Fear have his way. What would be next after the forty million? X knew the type. He wouldn't simply disappear and never be heard from again. If Doctor Fear were as smart as X thought he was, he would use the money to finance more experiments, possibly designing even more vile weaponry worse than what he already had. The consequences of giving this villain what he wanted could be catastrophic.

X reflected in wonder at how the times have changed. Back in the twenties, all he had to worry about were simple gangsters, men trying to make a living by selling illegal commodities. They weren't anti-American and they weren't out to destroy anything. Their ambitions were simply money-related. Some sought power, but only to further their goals of living life the way they saw it within the American ideal.

Lately, it seemed every threat X faced had a greater impact on a national or even international level. These types of threats are what the Department of Justice foresaw. They are what prompted the shadowy government official, K-9, to give him his mandate of acting outside the confines of the law. It was a mandate to protect the very law to which he as an operative, to get the job done, couldn't always adhere. The irony was not lost on Secret Agent X. It only made him try harder.

X pulled up to 383 Pearl Street, the headquarters for Brooklyn College. Somewhere inside this building was a clue to whom this Doctor Fear character was and what he really wanted. X was determined to find it.

Something clicked within Betty's memory. There was a story about a murder in the *Herald* months earlier that was unsolved. The Dean of Brooklyn College was found dead in a laboratory. It was written by a colleague of hers who lived just a few blocks from the hospital.

She walked the streets in the dead of night, glancing all around in a near paranoid fugue state. In the darkness the fear was returning and she had to keep reminding herself that it wasn't real. It was induced. It was forced upon her. *Remember the innocent boy. Remember Secret Agent X.*

As she repeated this mantra, she suddenly looked up to find herself in front of her colleague's brownstone house. His name was Henry Smith, or Hank as he like to be called. Betty wasn't sure what kind of reaction she would get from Hank. He was let go about three months ago and didn't have kind parting words for anyone in the office on his way out. He made a point that a woman should not be working when a man needed a job. Betty hoped he was just frustrated and didn't really have anything against her personally.

Her fears increasing, Betty gulped and knocked on the door. There was no answer. She insistently knocked louder, bludgeoning her fist on the hard wood door until pain shot up her arm. Frustrated, she turned the knob. The door opened with a slight creak.

"Hello?" she called out, nervous.

No answer came so she walked in, peering around a parlor in disarray. It was dark, the street lamps outside barely making a dent in the wall of enveloping black. It was enough to realize the outline of a floor lamp, though, so she waded through empty bottles and discarded deli wraps to turn it on.

She gasped as she saw Hank's body face down on the floor. Drool pooled around his lips, flowing into the wispy hair flopped over an otherwise bald head.

"Hank!" she yelled. She ran over to him and tried to awaken him. Checking his pulse, she was relieved to see he was still alive. "Hank, wake up," she said as she lightly shook his shoulder. Shaking him more roughly at his lack of response, she still got no result, so she went into the kitchen.

Taken aback by the rancid smell of dirty dishes and strewn trash, Betty managed to find a glass without too much grime on it. She turned on the faucet and jumped out of the way as water mixed with pockets of air sputtered out of the nozzle, ricocheted off a pan and sprayed in the air. The piping jerked up and down as the air in the lines forced its way out and finally allowed a steady stream. She filled the glass and ran back into the parlor.

Sitting Hank up for best effect, Betty hurled the water right into his face. The splash induced a mumble at best. This was going to take more drastic measures. Closing all the shades so as not to disturb the neighbors, she turned on every light in the house. Next, she lit a fire, making sure the vents were clean so she wouldn't smoke the room out.

Back in the kitchen, she managed to dig up some coffee beans. She ground them into a fine powder and boiled some water on the stove. She rolled up the cleanest paper she could find, put the ground coffee inside the cone and poured the hot water through it into a cup. It wouldn't be the best tasting coffee ever made, but it would serve its purpose.

By this time the parlor was very hot, enough to make her sweat. She saw that Hank was sweating in his sleep and beginning to stir. She splashed some more water on him and held the brewed coffee under his nose. His eyes slowly opened.

"Martha?" he asked. "Martha, you came back."

"Drink some of this," Betty commanded.

He sipped at the still steaming brew. "Oh," he winced. "That's awful. You still make the worst coffee ever."

"Open your eyes, Hank," Betty said. "I'm not your wife and I'm running out of time."

"What?" Hank blinked, the world coming into focus for the first time in a very long time. Betty gave him a minute to take in his surroundings.

"What are you doing here?" he asked.

"I need to ask you some questions," she spit out. She sat on the other side of the coffee table, tapping her fingernails on the arm of the chair.

"Why the hell would I tell you anything, missy?" he moaned. "You practically cost me my job." He climbed up onto the couch, put his head back and sniffed at the coffee.

"Because I need your help," she pleaded. "Because there's a maniac on the loose in the city and he needs to be brought in. And I did not cost you your job. You did."

"Look," he snarled, his eyes focusing hard. "Leave me alone. Can't you see I'm miserable?"

"Hank," Betty said, becoming more sympathetic. "What happened to you? You were a good reporter. Don't tell me my small amount of articles did this to you. Any paper in the city would have been glad to have you on their staff."

Hank hung his head, defeated. "What do you want to know?"

Betty wasted no time. "About two months ago, you wrote the piece on the death of Dean Withers from Brooklyn College. In the article you stated that the coroner had trouble explaining the cause of death and that there were currently no suspects. Yet, the next day a professor was reported missing. I remember that because I asked you then if it was related."

"What did I tell you?" Hank asked, sipping his coffee and grimacing at the taste. He laid back on the couch and closed his eyes in an attempt to clear his head.

"You told me to get lost and leave the reporting to able-bodied men."

"Ouch," Hank grimaced. "Sorry about that. You're not so bad, for a dame."

"Never mind that," Betty pressed. "What's the true story behind the Dean's death?"

"The coroner was just about to declare a homicide. Then an order comes down from the top. And when I say the top, I'm talking all the way. South. D.C., toots. I know. I was there when he got the call. No talking to the press. No declaration of cause of death. Just say it's unknown at this time. Old Timmy, he was right mad, he was. Can't stand the interference of government types. But what are you going to do?"

"Why the hush order?" Betty asked.

"Matter of national security," snorted Hank. "Or so the goons said. The President himself was here only the day before. I figure they didn't want any dirty laundry following Mr. Roosevelt around. Public image and all that. You follow?"

"Yes," Betty said. "I certainly do. But who was the missing professor?"

"Oh, yeah," Hank quipped. He seemed to come alive a bit when focusing on telling the story. The old reporter in him still craving the rush. "Furchtohne was his name. Some sort of science genius immigrant type. You know the kind. They run away from home and think they deserve a hand out because of their big brains, then turn all bitter when they realize they have to work for a living like everyone else."

Betty laughed. She wished things could have been different with Hank. He seemed like a good person when he didn't have a chip on his shoulder.

"Whatever happened to him?" She asked.

"Don't know," he said. "All the records were destroyed, or so I was told."

She stood up. "I have to go, Hank. Thank you for your help. I hope things work out better for you."

"Yes," Hank sighed. "Better. Well, that could only happen if Martha came back to me."

"If you want things to change, you have to change them yourself. That's what my mother always said."

Hank stared into the fire as she walked out the door.

Secret Agent X sat down in frustration. How could a college less than a decade old amass such a large body of paperwork? He had been searching through files half the night and hadn't found what he needed. This was obviously a dead end. Doctor Fear had covered his tracks well.

Then he heard footsteps down the hall. He shuttered his lamp and listened. A sharp, clicking noise echoed through the building, the sound of solid heels striking a hard wood floor with determined precision. He hid, blending in with the darkness and scouting from an advantageous corner. The weight of the stranger's tread and resounding harsh click of the shoe clued X in to the feminine nature of his visitor. It wasn't the light tap of high heels, but a working shoe, for comfort. The door to the office he was scrounging through opened and the lights came on. X started with surprise.

"Betty?" he gasped.

"There you are," she said.

"What are you doing here?" he asked. "How did you get released?" He couldn't believe what he was seeing. This is the same woman that mere hours ago he left in a panicked state on a hospital bed.

"Never mind that," she stated, all business. "You won't find what you need here. The man you're looking for is called Furchtohne. He was an immigrant professor. If you still have connections with your government friends, you might want to give them a call. My contact said all his records were destroyed. But we know better."

"By God, you're beautiful," X said. He kissed her full on the lips and left the office.

"Harvey, come in," X said into the receiver.

"Yes, boss," Harvey's crackling voice came over the speaker. His voice was slurred, groggy.

"Sorry to wake you, friend, but it's time for plan 42."

"Got it," Harvey said, then cut the transmission.

They met in a discreet, dark alley, a prearranged place that wasn't on most maps and wasn't named. Not a word was spoken out loud. They stood face to face, staring at each other's working mouths, reading the lips that made no sound but said so much.

Use the network for all it's worth, X mimed. *I need all the records available on a Brooklyn College professor named Furchtohne. He was only there a few months before disappearing. You still have your friend in the secret service?*

Yes, Harvey nodded.

Send them to me over the wire. I'll be waiting. We don't have much time.

Harvey left in a rush.

Thanks to many years of building an entire network of operatives throughout the nation, Secret Agent X had the information he needed within six hours.

Later, in his private lab, Secret Agent X was amazed at the information before him. This man, now calling himself Doctor Fear and quite clearly insane, was truly a genius. His work on sound technology and brain patterns were way above and beyond anything he had seen before. X considered himself a good scientist, but even he was baffled by some of these findings. The information wasn't complete, which didn't help. It handicapped his intentions for creating an antidote for the condition Fear's device induced, but he might be able to counter the beam if he could discern its direction and origin.

Next, he needed to determine where and when Fear would strike next. From the information Harvey supplied, X knew Fear's habits tended toward old world structures and mannerism. Beyond his work, he preferred antiquity over modern. Ideas of democracy and equality would still be foreign to him. He also knew Fear was hell-bent on revenge. Where would he strike?

While he worked, X kept the radio tuned into a news station as a low grade sound deterrent and as a way to keep informed of recent events. He was making progress on a muffled headpiece when his ears suddenly perked up in rapt attention at the sound of his president speaking.

"...the Mayor of New York comes to Washington, I tremble, because it means he wants something, and he almost always gets it. This project is killing two birds with one stone. It is not only putting to work thousands of people who need work, but it also is improving educational facilities now and for generations to come. There has been much suffering in this depression, but much good also has come out of it. It has given an opportunity to better conditions for the young people. I am interested in all projects for the improvement of education, and my wish for Brooklyn

College is the fine future it deserves. May it live to build a better American citizenship."

The voice changed to that of the announcer.

"That was several months ago when President Roosevelt helped lay the cornerstone for the new gymnasium at Brooklyn College. Today, College President Boylan will commemorate the founding of the college in a small ceremony to symbolize the goal of providing higher education to all citizens, rich or poor...'"

X tuned out the rest. That was it. If Fear wanted revenge against his former employers, he would get it there. The mayor of New York would be there as well as several high profile representatives from Washington.

Secret Agent X quickly finished up his work and left.

It is too quiet!

Doctor Fear listened intently through his latest invention. It was a sound wave modifier that was tuned to receive the tone and pitch only of the human voice. Once Fear had latched onto Secret Agent X and his network of informants, he was able to ascertain his plans and counter his moves. But for the past six hours, everything had gone silent. This frustrated Fear to no end. It meant the secret agent was on to him, had found a counter. No matter. He couldn't stop what was coming. Doctor Fear's revenge was destiny made manifest.

Doctor Fear looked around at his handiwork and smiled with pride. From the scavenged remains of his lab in Brooklyn College and the debris he discovered lying around in the subway tunnel system, he had built from scratch a secret home base right beneath the feet of the people he wished to destroy. After weeks of wandering and surviving on scraps, he had discovered many secret passages and abandoned areas down here. He memorized them and made them his home, culminating in what was probably the best scientific research lab in the city, one to which only he had access. New inventions sprang to mind as well, though nothing on the level of Soundbreaker.

He had improved his wardrobe as well. Now dressed all in black, he sported a cape that flared out under his rising arms. His boots were a new invention that dispersed the sounds he made walking in awkward directions. Maneuvering his cape allowed him to direct the sounds to create an audio effect where and how he wanted.

His helmet was made from an old gas mask. He removed the canister pouch from the face and centered the seal over the ears rather than the nose and mouth. This required him to shave off all his hair so the seal would hold. Inside the pouches were special noise filters. They made sure he wouldn't become victim to his own Soundbreaker as well as enhancing his listening capabilities. He could adjust the levels of both reception and protection via a series of dials behind each earpiece.

All fitted out with his gear, Doctor Fear left his lair and headed out to make his claim on the world.

A thick miasmic fog clung to the school grounds like a spider's web. No matter how much you brushed away, loose strands would always be left behind. It reduced visibility and caused a subliminal tension in those who had to work in it. Workers set up tables and chairs and put together a forty-foot stage complete with curtains and a podium.

As a hired hand, Secret Agent X knew his way around a work crew. His years of experience as a sailor taught him how to keep his head down, work hard, and stay unnoticed. His disguise was that of an Italian immigrant who knew little English and was slightly overweight. He was wearing coveralls which gave him plenty of pockets, both inside and out, to hide his various cache of weapons and other useful items. The overweight look he sported was actually a condition of all his equipment and the padding he used to keep it safe. It raised his body temperature and made him sweat profusely, but that only served to enforce the stereotype he was portraying.

X consistently scanned the crowd, looking for any sign of Doctor Fear. He knew Fear would most likely have his own cache of gadgets, so he looked for those telltale signs of someone carrying things and trying to hide it. All morning this activity went on. He finally finished rigging up the stage curtains. The crowd grew to about four thousand. The speakers were set to begin soon, starting with the mayor. There was still no sign of Doctor Fear. Could he have guessed wrong about Fear's intentions?

The time was here. The mayor approached the podium and began his speech about new tomorrows and educating the young, eager masses. The crowd was unusually quiet. They all seemed blissfully eager to attend to what the mayor was saying. The first few hundred in the front were particularly intent, their eyes unblinking and their heads nodding in a near circular motion. Something was wrong.

X unfastened one of his ear plugs for a moment. The droning of the mayor's words struck him like an impact. He turned his head towards the speaker and began to focus on the speech. Almost nonchalantly he placed the earpiece back in. Instantly his mind snapped out of the near-trance. Sub-sonics! Fear was here and he was broadcasting a low-wave frequency, turning the crowd into submissive sheep.

X needed a better angle to view the crowd. He dashed behind the stage curtain and began climbing up one of the ropes, hand over hand. Reaching the top he brushed aside the curtain's edge and spied the crowd from above. There! Moving slowly to the front was a man with a hood dressed all in black. X scrambled back down the rope, narrowly avoiding tearing his hands to shreds from rope burn. He dashed to the front of the stage.

Doctor Fear lifted Soundbreaker and fired.

X leapt in front of the mayor, unveiling a retractable fan that expanded to the size of a large shield. Based upon the Japanese war fans of centuries ago, the blades acted like a phonogram that dispersed sound in a broader, less focused direction. The waves of sound deflected off the fan and struck the front of the crowd. The entranced front row stopped their mindless bobbing and immediately screamed in fear. The ensuing chaos of their panicked cries and efforts to run away snapped the rest of the crowd out of their stupor and started a confused jumble of jostling and shouting.

"Mr. Mayor, are you all right?" X checked.

The mayor nodded. "Who are you?"

"Just a concerned citizen," X replied and then took off into the crowd.

He spied Doctor Fear making a dash toward the street. He had the advantage in that people cleared out of his way in haste as he waved Soundbreaker before him in a sweeping motion, causing more mass panic. X had to fight through a rushing crowd for every inch of ground he had to make up against Fear's head start. He sidestepped crazed plebeians as well as sobbing intellectuals. He used various blocking and take-down maneuvers just to avoid getting hit or trampled. Several times he lost sight of Fear but kept moving in the direction of where people were running from, considering Fear's sound technology was the source of the distress. Here and there he would catch a glimpse of the trailing black cloak and continue his sojourn through a sea of distorted faces.

Finally, the crowd thinned out as X came out onto one of Brooklyn's main thoroughfares. Dashing down Willoughby Avenue, X made a beeline to the Subway stop at the corner of Myrtle where he spotted his quarry racing down the stairs. As he rushed around the corner, suddenly he was overcome with a wave of sound so intense it nearly knocked him off his feet. Doctor Fear had hidden behind a trash can and hopped up at the last second to pull the trigger on Soundbreaker. He held nothing back, placing all the settings on full power. Secret Agent X went down like a puppet whose strings were cut.

Doctor Fear laughed maniacally.

"Now you see the true power of fear!" he sneered. "You ridiculous Americans pretend to live in your stupid dream without looking at the realities right under your noses! I knew it was a mistake to come here as soon as I saw your unwashed masses huddled beneath your precious Lady Liberty," all this he spat with contempt. "Your democracy is a lie. It is nothing!"

Secret Agent X heard all this as if in a long tunnel. The protection he had in his ears had saved his hearing. It had probably saved his very life. The concussive force was no less brutal though, and he played possum on the ground while his enemy ranted madly in German.

"Soon," Fear continued. "The Fascist regime my countrymen so mistakenly embraced will run its course. The rise of reason and science will be heralded by the red masses now embracing a more socialist cause, a cause that lifts science above such petty concerns as ideology and superstition. Socialism will embrace us. It will make all society richer by far. I know now I went the wrong way when I boarded that boat all those years ago. I should have gone east. Your democracy is nothing!"

"No," X ground through clenched teeth. The pain was nearly unbearable. Fear's weapon was even more powerful than X thought possible. If he hadn't prepared for this encounter, his brain would have been no better than jelly now. "I don't believe you."

"So," Fear laughed. "You still live. I knew you would have some protection. I've known your every move. You figured out a way to shut me out, but you didn't figure on the raw power I hold in my hands."

"Science and reason can be used with Democracy to make a better life for all." X was stalling, needing time to gather his wits, get his strength back. He felt the slightest tremor in the ground. The feel of a train approaching.

"Wrong!" Fear took the bait. "Science, in its very endeavor, is communism. The control of nature and even man himself is the full conscious expression of human society!"

X snickered, mocking Fear's diatribe. "You are merely quoting an asinine book. Is that the best you can do? You are a nothing. A nobody. A bitter man who couldn't take the hits life threw his way. You lash out at the world like a petulant child."

Fear screamed in rage. In his anger he brought Soundbreaker right up to X's head.

That's just what X was ready for. He brought his fist up with all his reserve strength and knocked the deadly device right out of Fear's hands. It clattered away, off the platform and onto the tracks. At that point the subway train stormed through the tunnel, shattering the device into a thousand pieces.

"No!" Fear cried.

The train stopped and Fear jumped on the train when the doors were opened. Secret Agent X tried to get up and follow but stumbled as his legs gave way. He was still too weak from the sound blast.

In a haze he realized that someone was helping him up. He remembered hands lifting him, people asking if he needed a doctor, and shrugging them off, informing them he needed to get on that train. It came through to him like a dream, as though he were running through mud that never let him get anywhere. There was some jostling and shoving, people getting angry that he wouldn't let them help, others calling for police, one man exclaiming there was blood coming out of his ear.

He didn't care. He had to get on that train.

Finally, the door shut behind him and he sat down for just a minute to gather his wits. As he looked around and realized where he was, he saw a few faces staring at him in consternation. He must look a horrid sight. The train lurched into motion and the ancient bedrock of the subway tunnels zoomed by in a mesmerizing chaotic pattern.

As awareness began to return, Secret Agent X remembered who and what he was, and why he was here. He reached into his jacket and retrieved a small bottle of pills. Popping the cover he quickly swallowed down one of the equilibrium tracers. Within a few moments, the chemical agent did its work and helped him center himself. Now he could track down Doctor Fear and put an end to his terror.

Moving with renewed determination, X opened the back door of the moving rail car. Stepping over the connecting links, X balanced himself out on the crossbeams while the rocking cars zoomed over the tracks. He had to pry open the door to the next car from the outside using a large nail file as a wedge. Fingers aching from the effort, he pried enough space to get a good handhold and open the door. Just then the train lurched around a bend and sent his feet out from under him. He grabbed onto the sliding door with all his might and held on for dear life as it slid open and carried him to the side of the rail car. He barely managed to hook his shoe tips on a window frame to avoid flying out and smashing into the hard granite walls of the tunnel.

Inch by agonizing inch X crawled along the side of the car until he was fully inside. He looked up and realized he was in the engine car. There were no passengers in here. He walked up to the control area to talk to the operator. On his way there, he noticed a shoe sticking out from under one of the seats. Bending down to inspect further he saw the shoe belonged to a body dressed as a subway train operator.

X suddenly realized in horror who was driving the train.

"Fear! Stop!" he shouted.

"Never," Fear returned. "This paltry American engineering is all too easy to tamper with. I'm afraid our train is on a one way trip to hell."

"No!" X leapt at him, hoping to stop whatever tinkering the genius scientist was doing to the controls. He grabbed him by his black cape and yanked him bodily out of the control area. Fear slid halfway down the aisle. X stared at the controls, perplexed by the configuration in front of him.

"What have you done?" he asked.

"It's too late," Fear intoned through his mask. "This train is doomed." He got up and made a dash toward the open back door.

Growling in frustration, X studied the re-configuration of wiring and mechanical controls. He finally decided that whatever Fear had done would be worse than having no control at all, so he began ripping out various wires and switches and hoping for the best. He tried to engage the emergency stop but nothing happened. The brake was loosed from its moors. He believed he stopped Fear's sabotage, but stopping the train was another problem that couldn't be solved here. There was nothing to do but warn the passengers.

Secret Agent X made a dash back through the door and into the other car. He noticed that the back door to this car was open and that people were yelling in surprise from the next car over. He traversed the crossbeams into that one and saw that one man was down in the aisle with a bleeding head.

"What happened?" he asked.

"A man," answered one woman. "Dressed all in black came through here. He was wild and had on a strange mask. He said we were all going to die. This man rose to confront him and the dark man shot some kind of loud blast out of his hand, almost like a gun shot, then he went through there."

She pointed at the exit hatch at the end of the train.

"Warn everyone," X said. "The train is out of control and will crash. You need to brace yourselves and prepare for impact."

"Who are you?"

"A friend."

X went to the hatch and held up his war fan as he exited, expecting an attack at any moment. He looked out at the tracks racing below, wondering where Fear had gone. There was a ladder next to the hatch that went up onto the roof. He climbed it.

The blow struck almost immediately. He barely got the fan up in time to deflect a sonic shot at close range. Fear had some sort of device that allowed him to project a ball of compressed sound that exploded like a gunshot on impact. Though the fan deflected the initial impact, the wave of sound still washed over him. Lancing pain assaulted his eardrums yet again. His protective devices allowed him to withstand it, but tears streamed from his eyes regardless.

Fear, lying flat on the roof of the car to avoid the stone ceiling rushing by, crawled up to X to finish him off. He was exultant with victory. He smashed X's hand with his sling shooter. X grimaced in pain but held on through sheer determination.

With a desperate grab, X reached up and took hold of a handful of black cape. He dragged Fear forward, bringing his face right up to the oddly designed gas mask. With savage fury his teeth tore at the rubbery material and yanked the hood cockeyed.

Fear cried out and tore the rest of his contraption off, exposing his bald pate. He raised his gun for a final blow to the exposed head of Secret Agent X. Before it could land though, he was torn right off the roof.

The out of control train had finally come to the end of its track. It smashed into an enclosed, bricked-up section of an unused tunnel. Scattering brick and mortar everywhere, the train slammed to a sudden halt. Metal twisted and crunched together like a tin drum crushed by a front end loader. The front car was hanging over the bay where the tunnel ended.

Secret Agent X slowly came back to consciousness. The impact of the crash had knocked him out cold but his natural fortitude and resilience had allowed him to unconsciously hold on. Looking at his surroundings, X noticed that people were moving inside the car. That was a good sign.

They would be able to help each other out. He saw no trace of Doctor Fear.

He climbed down off the car and made his way over to the rubble of the bricked-up wall. Choking on dust and debris, he worked his way through the chaos until he came to the opening over the bay. The front hung out about twenty feet, the strong iron crossbeams and pins keeping it from disconnecting from the rest of the train and plunging into the cold water another twenty feet below.

Looking out over the edge of the precipice, X saw Doctor Fear dangling by one arm, trying to claw his way back up. Fear was hanging onto the cliff face, his suit was nearly torn off of him. X saw that he was losing his grip and was not going to make it.

"Give me your hand!" X shouted. He reached down but couldn't quite grasp the man's arm. Fear looked up, his eyes glossy with the pain of struggle. X could see nothing now but an old bitter man, someone who was beaten by the trials and travails he had gone through and was now trying to take it out on the world.

"No," Fear coughed. "I'll never accept help from one such as you."

"Don't be a fool!" X cried. "You'll die!"

"So be it," Fear whispered, and let go.

"No!" X shouted.

Fear made no sound as he dropped into the bay.

"They never found a body," Betty said to Secret Agent X, back in his guise as A.J. Martin, as they walked along the pier.

"Yes," replied X. "I know. I was a part of the search, unknown to any others. There isn't much possibility he survived that, but I would like to be certain. For your piece of mind more than anything else."

"You don't have to worry about me anymore, tough guy," Betty replied, smiling. "I'm quite the capable gal, I'll have you know."

"Yes," X smiled back. "You certainly are."

"I hear the hospital received a mysterious donation in the form of an antidote to the effects of Fear's terror. You wouldn't happen to know anything about that, would you?" Betty asked.

"Always a reporter," X grinned. "But it is not an antidote. It is only a curative mixture to treat most of the symptoms. The only antidote will be time and determination that I know of. The latter of which you seemed to master quite well."

"Give me your hand!" X shouted.

As they walked, X noticed a quick flash of light on the Brooklyn Bridge over the river.

"It is time for me to go," he informed Betty.

"So soon?" she asked, already knowing the answer.

X simply nodded, knowing he didn't need to explain his duty to her. The signal was one of his operatives letting him know that his presence was required at one of his many hideouts. No doubt, if he was in his car, he already would have heard from Harvey.

"Farewell, Betty," he said and ran off into the night.

THE END

Author's Dedication –
To my Dad, Henry (Hank) A. Courtemanche 1942-2010
A pulp reader, Lone Ranger and Tarzan fan, and an inspiration to
write more stories. My thanks to you for life and love.

EXPLORING FEAR

Sometimes, stories take their time in the telling. They come at us one way and then develop another. Every story I take on is like sparring with a friend, you get hit back and every once in a while it hurts. When that happens, you tend to want to take it easy for awhile and maybe spar with someone else.

In 2008, when writing my first Secret Agent X story (currently available in Secret Agent X Volume 3), I took a short break from it to start another one. I wanted to explore Betty's character a bit more and I wanted to write something a little darker. I finished chapter one in a rush. It came pouring out of me with incredible energy and felt really good. It was like sparring with someone new for the first time. Both of us performed well and no one got hurt.

I then went back and finished my first story. That took the punch out of me for some time. About six months later I returned to the ring and began sparring with my new partner again. This time it was more measured, a work out with a pace and a goal. There was research to do, characters to develop and plot lines to weave. I needed to focus on the consistent tone that I had established in that first chapter.

My first Secret Agent X story had our hero going out and exploring the world. This new one is more internal, a discovery of inner reserves of strength, of overcoming our fears and doing what needs to be done. I wanted to explore fear, not just of scary villains, but of those intangible things: fear of the future, fear of the unknown, and probably the most paralyzing of all, fear of failure.

Overcoming these things is, of course, what makes Secret Agent X a hero, but that's expected of him. The greater feat of heroism I laid at the feet of Betty. Although she's shown great resolve in helping out X in the past, I wanted to put her through the ringer and make her a hero in her own right rather than a resourceful sidekick. I hope I succeeded in giving her the spotlight she deserves.

Eventually, the story has to come back to Secret Agent X. It's his book, after all. I'd like to thank Ron Fortier for his suggestions when it came to creating the villain of the story. I didn't use them all but they sparked the creativity needed for a villain people could root against yet still have some kind of empathy for. I hope I created a villain people will remember. The implications of what he could have done had his plan succeeded are truly frightening if you really think about it. Doctor Fear indeed!

I found it fascinating that subway rail cars haven't changed that much over the years until very recently. Or, I should say, how advanced they were in the 1930s. They were a beacon of modern progress and their durability is a testament to the excellent engineering of the times. The pseudo-science of both Doctor Fear and Secret Agent X are the fun things to play with in the story, but it shouldn't overshadow the accomplishments of real science at the time. After all, it was real science which fueled the imaginations of writers in the 1930s to create such make-believe in the first place.

Pseudo-science also ties into the age-old fear of technological advancement, which is actually just a basic fear of change. People fear change because change brings with it the unknown, the unfamiliar, and the possible inability to deal with it. Secret Agent X is a character who, on the surface, is opposed to change. He's trying to maintain the status quo. He fights for his country because he wants to keep his country the way it is, keep it on the same path. But what if that path is a path of continual change, advancement? Are you then opposed to change, or an agent of change? I would say, in the case of Secret Agent X, it is the latter. Since he is a stalwart fellow he would not be subject to the same fears that grip the mortal hearts of others. That's what this story is all about: The hero defeating fear. I'm done sparring with this story now. Time to put on my gloves for another. I hope you enjoyed it!

This one's for you, Mom! You're the best!

H. JARROD COURTEMANCHE is a Veteran of the U.S. Airforce. He graduated from UMASS/Lowell with a bachelors degree in Liberal Arts. He has written many short stories and has written and directed short films for Mindbeside Studios (www.mindbeside.com).

SECRET AGENT "X"

A Stygian Unkindness

by Kevin Noel Olson

Clutching the wheel with the same unconscious violence with which he clenched his teeth, Carlos 'Swifty' Marconi examined every inch of the street, his eyes dancing from shadowed façade to flickering streetlamp. Sweat crawled over his brow. Six more blocks! Swifty felt sure; six blocks, and he'd be safe! He allowed a nervous smile to adorn his lips for a second. "Five," he said aloud as he drove across Poll Avenue. Bristling at the sound of his own voice, Carlos snapped his lips closed and looked about. He sighed and shook his head. Relaxed a bit, his brow furrowed to concentrate on the next five blocks. Five more blocks to stay alive!

Swifty's green sedan rolled slowly through the night. The tops of the tall buildings disappeared into the black sky overhead. Though no competing traffic or pedestrians wandered the street, Swifty stopped the automobile at each intersection before continuing. The city's cold breath wrapped the vehicle in a fetid aroma. Dank, unpaved alleyways hid their secrets in impenetrable darkness.

Carlos pulled his cigarette case out and removed a cigarette. He pushed it between trembling lips and struck a match on the dash. The flame danced as he pulled it to the cigarette and sucked in its soothing smoke. He sighed and leaned back as the sedan swam easily across Borderland Street.

Every muscle pulled taut as a raven-shaped shadow glided noiselessly in front of the crescent moon and fell across the windshield. "Damn!" he expelled. He punched the gas as he stared upward through the windshield. The stars twinkled in black sky, disappearing and reappearing rapidly as the man-sized raven of darkness blocked them out.

Drawing the tobacco smoke into his lungs, Swifty reached into his jacket. He pulled out his snub-nose .38 revolver. He looked at the weapon and let out a chuckle. Great for killing somebody at close range and keeping in a pocket, he doubted he could hit a target flying above him in the dark. He slammed on the brakes and scanned the night air.

He watched as the stars disappeared again in waves washing toward him in the black ocean of the night sky. His left hand held the gun outside the car's window. Shaking, he aimed his revolver at the speeding darkness. His gloved hand pulled the trigger. The .38 released hot lead and sparks along with the cacophonous report.

The dark, bird-like figure lit up momentarily as bullets left its location and tore into the sedan. The Tommy Gun rattled loudly as the orange flashes escaped the barrel, accenting the frightening vision.

Bullets ripped into the hood, spraying green paint and metal from the vehicle's surface. The windshield exploded in a dazzling spray of glass. Carlos swallowed his cigarette as the bullets tore into him. He coughed and spurted blood as flames sprang from the back seat. The machine gun fell silent as Swifty slumped against the wheel. The bird figure disappeared into the blackness.

A light came to Swifty's vision. Was he dead? He sure felt awful, but no. Death can't hurt like this, he decided. He didn't figure you bled as much either. He looked at his right arm, now useless and bleeding. He noticed the blood under his jacket near the chest and stomach. He coughed, ejecting the broken and wet cigarette from his lungs with a stream of ash. He blinked crimson liquid from his eyes and put the car in gear. "Four blocks," he said aloud in his shocked daze. "Four blocks."

His mind set on a goal, he rolled the car slowly and erratically down the street. "Three blocks," he muttered mechanically.

The cold night air pulled at his wounds. He punched the horn. "Come on, you bulls! Where's a cop when you need 'em?" He laughed aloud. He choked on red liquid spurting from his lips. He retrieved another cigarette. He held the papered tobacco in the flames from the seat behind him. Police lights and sirens invaded the night ahead of him. "There you fellers are," he said with a grin. "I've never been happy to see coppers before." His head fell against the horn, and it wailed into the night.

The first police car rushed to the green sedan as fire licked the back seat and threatened to spread. The passenger door popped open and detective John Burks sprang out like a jack-in-the-box His tie flew over his overcoat as he pushed back the brim of his slouch hat. He threw his cigarette into the gutter as a uniformed officer rushed out of the driver's side. "Holy mack-an'-all!" Burks exclaimed as he rushed to the burning car. "Move it, Webbing! We've gotta get that guy outta there!"

The second police car wailed to announce its presence and it screeched to a halt next to the first. Burks and Webbing struggled to pull open the locked driver's door on the sedan open. "Hey, mac!" Burks said as he waved the officer over that escaped from the second police car. "Get over here and help us pull!"

Carrying a fire extinguisher, the officer rushed over and set it on the ground. Instead of pulling on the door he crawled through the destroyed windshield past the unconscious Carlos and pulled at the lock.

Burks and Webbing pulled the door open with unexpected ease, sending them to the pavement. The moment almost carried a Keystone Cops demeanor, though dampened by the gravity of the moment. The horn stopped blaring as Carlos spilled onto the street. The officer extracted himself from the windshield and retrieved the extinguisher. Burks and Webbing rushed to save Carlos' life as the other officer sprayed the white chemical on the fire.

"Get your belt off!" Burks shouted to Webbing as he removed the cinch from his overcoat and tied it tight around Carlos' bleeding arm. "We've gotta stop the tomato juice or this guy's just dry soup!"

Obediently, Webbing removed his belt as Burks threw his overcoat over Carlos and started wrapping him tight. The other officer returned to his car and used his radio to phone the hospital. "Hey, John," he shouted. Burks looked at him as the officer shouted "catch!" and threw a black bag at the detective.

Burks caught the first aid kit and opened it quickly, retrieving bandages and alcohol. Carlos regained consciousness and looked at the officers through a bloodied face. "Watch out for the Ravenmen," Carlos strained to whisper. "They'll get me!"

Burks shook his head. "Nothin' doin', mac." He wrapped a handkerchief around his hand and soaked it from one of the bottles. He held it over Carlos' mouth and nose. Carlos passed out. "One thing I learned as a medic in the war," Burks said to Webbing, "is you ain't gonna be able to save a brother's life if he's awake."

Burks and Webbing worked quickly to stop the bleeding. Sweat poured from Burks' brow as he worked deftly with a needle and thread to stitch up the bullet wounds. He gritted his teeth in a trance. The rest of the world didn't exist for him. Saving a life was all that mattered.

Ambulance sirens filled the night air as Burks blessed the city planners for putting the hospital close to the police station. Burks turned to see the other police car pull into the night. He frowned as he looked at the gold star painted on the door. Instead of the name of the town the door sported a large, black 'X.'

Burks stole a moment to shake his fist after the car. "X, you belly-crawlin' coward! Ya better run!"

Burks bristled as he looked back at Carlos and Webbing. He had to stay. He pulled a cigarette from Carlos' shirt pocket and looked at Webbing. "Get me lit!" he growled.

Webbing fumbled through his pockets until he produced a lighter. He struck the flame to life and put it to the cigarette. Burks drank the smoke

"Get your belt off!" Burks shouted *."We've gotta stop the tomato juice or this guy's just dry soup!"*

as though it were coffee. The ambulance arrived on the scene. Burks and Webbing moved away as the white-clad medics knelt by Carlos.

The driver pointed out the symbol of a red cross on the front of his round, white cap to Burks. "What happened here? Looks like this guy's been through a war zone!"

Burks nodded. "Sure, 'cept I don't see no doughboys here. We ain't got a clue. We heard the horn honkin' an' we came out to cite him for disturbin' the peace." The detective shrugged. "When we got here, we found this guy ain't got many pieces left to 'im."

The driver worked on Carlos without looking at Burks. "Looks like he went over the top of the trench," he muttered.

"You were in the war?" Burks asked before shaking his head. "Don't matter. It sure looks like a machine gun the way he's tore up. It turned the sedan into a spaghetti sieve."

The driver nodded. "Looks like an airplane the way the roof's been chewed."

Burks examined the sedan with his eyes. "Yeah," he nodded. "Shoulda seen that. Gotta be above the car to do that."

"Did you hear a plane?" the other medic asked.

Burks looked at Webbing. Webbing shrugged. "No, I didn't hear nothin'."

The ambulance driver shrugged. "Well, it wasn't a pigeon. They can't carry a Thompson." He nodded his head at the other medic.

The medic went to the ambulance and opened the back door. He looked over at the policemen as he began to pull out a stretcher. "Hey, help me out here, fellas."

Webbing hopped into the ambulance and grabbed the other end of the stretcher. "This thing looks ancient," he said as he held poles of the stretcher.

"Yeah?" the medic replied. "The city hardly coughs up for gas. It was up to them, we'd carry this guy the whole way. I bet they buy you fellas your own bullets."

Webbing laughed. "No insult meant, buddy. I was just makin' a comment. I admire a sawbones what can make this stuff work."

They carried the stretcher to the sedan and laid it next to Carlos. The driver looked sideways at Burks and bent over with the other medic to lift the injured man onto the stretcher. "Nice to see ya help out, mac," he said to Burks.

Burks raised both hands. "Hey, I got a bad back." He threw his thumb toward the ambulance. "You don't have room in there for another passenger."

The driver let out a terse laugh. "Not if we can help it."

The medics lifted the stretcher carrying Carlos into the air. Burks followed them. "Do you need a police escort?"

The driver turned to Burks. "What? For five blocks? Come on!"

Burks turned to Webbing who greeted him with a shrug. Burks returned his eyes to the driver. "Have it your way, mac. No skin off my teeth."

They loaded Carlos and got into the ambulance. The vehicle pulled away as Burks and Webbing looked on. "Must be the end of their shift," Burks muttered. "They seem testy."

Webbing looked up suddenly as a whooshing sound filled the air. "Burks," he shouted and pointed his finger toward the sky. "Look!" The shape of a gigantic bird blotted out the stars as it moved after the ambulance, about twenty feet off the ground. Webbing pulled his gun and fired at the shape.

Burks shook his head as he pulled his .45. "You missed! Are you tryin' to win a kewpie or not?" He aimed carefully at the shape and fired.

The figure tilted harshly as the pistol rang out. The man in the flying suit wobbled and began to dive after the ambulance. It struck the back of the van with a violent *thud*. The driver stopped and got out.

"Get the car!" Burks shouted and Webbing jumped. He got in as Burks ran to the running board and climbed on. Webbing drove the car to the halted ambulance and stopped.

Burks walked over with the medic to the dark figure on the ground. It was a tall, thin man with wings of light, black metal. A Tommy-gun rested some feet from the figure. Blood flowed profusely from a small wound in the man's temple, staining his blonde hair and the dark wings.

"How about that?" Burks huffed. "This guy couldn't drop an enemy with a machine gun, but I drop him with a single shot." He knelt over the man as more of a formality than anything. Grabbing the man's wrist, Burks shook his head. "He's dead. I'd have aimed to wound if I couldn't seen anything at all. I don't get it. What's the game here?"

The driver shrugged. "All I know's if we don't get our patient to the hospital he might not make it." He returned to the ambulance and climbed into his seat.

"Wait a minute!" Burks shouted. "What about the body?"

The driver put his head out the open window as he slammed the door. "Call the mortuary." The wheels on the van turned as it moved away.

Webbing and Burks stared after it.

Burks turned to Webbing and nodded. "Get on the radio and call this into the station. Have them contact Chessler's Funeral Parlor." He looked at the body in front of him and shook his head. "He might appreciate the new customer."

Webbing went to the car and got on the radio. Burks scanned the area. Something moved in the darkness of the adjacent alley. Burks looked at Webbing. The uniformed officer spoke into the radio. Burks walked to the alley to investigate.

In a moment, Webbing left the car. Burks walked out of the alley and motioned him over. "Come on, Webbing," he said. "Let's get the stiff out of this paper airplane. We'll need it for evidence." Burks whistled as he looked down at the winged corpse. "I sure hope there ain't a gaggle of these guys."

"Looks like a raven costume, so it should be an unkindness of ravens. A gaggle is for geese." Burks grunted as Webbing looked at the body. "Shouldn't we wait for the mortician?"

Burks chewed his lip. "No, you idiot! We're the police! It's our job to figure out how a corpse got like it is, and mortician's job is to figure how to bury 'em!"

Burks clicked a black metal button on the man's chest. The straps connecting the wings to his back loosened. Burks took the arms out and turned to Webbing. "Help me roll him off."

They rolled the man off the wings. Burks found the reinforcing bars and collapsed them like an umbrella. "Nifty," Burks said as he admired the engineering. He turned to Webbing again. "Help me load 'em in the back seat."

They loaded the collapsed metal wings into the police car. "Give me the keys," Burks said and Webbing did.

Burks climbed into the driver's seat as Webbing looked on. "What am I supposed to do?"

Burks looked at him out the open car window. "Stay here until Chessler gets here. Think you can handle it?"

The young policeman nodded. Burks pulled away. Just as the car turned the corner two blocks away a voice rang out. "Stop him, you idiot!"

Webbing turned about, amazed to see Burks walk out of the alley. He looked after the disappearing car.

Burks stood next to Webbing and sighed. "That was Secret Agent X!"

A black, x-shaped spot of ink on Burks's cheek confirmed it for Webbing.

"You've got something on your face, sir."

Burks took his shiny revolver and looked at his reflection. "Yeah." He took his handkerchief out of his pocket. "Yeah," he sighed. "That's egg on my face, rookie. X's got the wings. He's behind all this!" He carelessly batted his palm with the barrel of his gun. "Even if he's not, I owe him a punch on the jaw!"

Betty Dale yawned and slipped her robe over her nightgown. The knock insisted on her walking into the thin light of dawn crawling through the window. The knock sounded again. "I'm coming!" she replied with disgust. She walked down the staircase of her two story home in slippers. She sneered at the portrait of her mother as she did so.

She walked toward the front door and opened it. A milkman smiled at her. "Hello, ma'am," he said politely. "Quite a morning isn't it?"

Betty pushed her blonde curls back. "What do you think?"

"Beautiful," the milkman replied. He looked at her face for a moment before turning to look at the sun-streaked sky and nodded. "It really is beautiful."

Betty yawned before crossing her arms. "Not as beautiful as the dream I was having," she replied, the dream of her and Secret Agent X, no longer a secret nor an agent. Not a mysterious X. He was no longer anything but her lover and companion on a sandy beach with nothing disguising him. Nothing but a romantic dream. That was her dream.

The milkman interrupted her reverie with a smile. "I have to arrange a milk delivery."

"What!? Now? At this ungodly hour?"

The milkman nodded. "Oh, rumor has it that he's awake at all hours of the day." He pulled a notepad and pencil from his pocket and stepped into the house.

Betty prepared to object until he wrote two lines on the pad where she could see. The figure of an 'X' is what he wrote. Even in her groggy condition she understood. She threw her arms around him with a smile. "Oh, it's you!"

He reached over and pushed the door shut. "Careful, Miss Dale! What will the neighbors think?"

She giggled and held him tight. "Someday they won't think anything."

He nodded as she released her arms. "A fond wish of mine, Betty. I could have been an agent of mine, you know."

Shaking her head, she said, "No. I saw your eyes."

Secret Agent X, in his milkman disguise, allowed a chuckle. "The windows of the soul are the hardest to disguise."

Betty put her hands on her hips. "Still, what on earth are you doing waking me up so early?"

"I need your help," X replied. "America needs your help."

Betty's brow furrowed. "Sounds serious. Anything I can do to help a great man and this great land, I will do. What do you need?"

X nodded. "That's why I came to you. I know you can be trusted. I need you to interview a prominent industrialist for your newspaper."

"You mean spy on him?"

X nodded in the affirmative. "Not exactly, but close. You just need to interview him while I watch and listen from an obscure point."

"Who is it?" Betty asked.

"He's not who he appears to be," X said. "Or, at least, he is not who he is currently impersonating. The man you are to interview is wearing the guise of a dead man. You are to interview Doctor Cormer."

Betty's eyes widened. "Doctor Cormer?"

"Is dead," X replied. "I am certain you are familiar with the metallurgical genius. He is being impersonated."

"By whom?"

X looked about the room, as if the security of their conversation were at risk. "You recall a master criminal in France during the early decade?"

Betty gasped. "You don't mean!"

X nodded. "I wish I didn't. A mastermind of strategy and an unmatched genius of disguise, he will prove to be extremely challenging."

Betty whispered the name harshly, her tone mixed with hate and fear. "Fantômas!"

"None other," the milkman replied as his expression twisted inhumanly. "Fantômas."

Betty watched as the eyes of Secret Agent X turned milky white. She screamed and moved toward the door as a gun appeared in the agent's hand and fired a stream of gas. "As I said, my dear, the windows of the soul are the hardest to disguise." He nodded. "X will challenge my designs. He will find the challenge most difficult with his beloved at my mercy!" A dark laugh rang throughout the house.

Burks walked through the door of the squad room with a cigar between his teeth. Without removing his ragged fedora, he squinted at the young officer searching the file cabinet. "What went to hell while I was asleep, Webbing?"

Webbing turned to the graceless and aged detective. "Hey, Detective Burks. Nothing new's crossed my desk since last night. It's been quiet, considering."

"Huh," Burks said between chewing on the cigar. Sparks flew off the end and to the granite floor. "Things usually go to hell when I'm not around. Something's gotta be goin' on."

Webbing stifled a sigh. "No ,sir. We did find out who the pigeon from hell shot up last night, but no I.D. on the Icarus that coughed bullets all over his car."

"Leave the witty banter to me, rookie," Burks said. "It takes years to perfect. Just tell me who got shot up."

Webbing nodded solemnly. "Yes, sir. It was a hired killer named Carlos Marconi. Goes by the name of Swifty."

"He wasn't Swift enough last night."

"I thought you said you'd perfected witty banter."

"Don't get fresh, punk. Did the hospital say how Swifty's makin' out?"

"Sounds like he'll live. I went over this morning and they've got him wrapped tighter than Karloff."

"Don't get obscure on me, either, Webbing. What the heck's a Karloff?"

"Boris Karloff is a screen actor, sir. Played The Mummy."

"Hah! Like I got time to go and watch the talkies when Secret Agent X is out there fowlin' everything up! He's up to something, mark my words. He took a squad car and evidence, too. He's a real-life monster!" Burks punctuated by biting the cigar in half. The lit half fell to the floor and released a spray of sparks, ashes, and smoke.

Webbing shrugged. "I went and saw The Mummy when I was a kid. Scared the pants off of me."

"I'm surprised your momma let you go."

Webbing shook his head. "She didn't. I snuck out to see it. Besides, I was fifteen."

"It scared ya that much when ya first saw it? Fifteen's nearly man-sized!"

"Scared me the first time I saw it and the fifth time I saw it, too. Great piece of celluloid, that one."

Burks crushed the still-lit cigar into the floor. "We've got our own pieces ta make into somethin', Webbing. We gotta get to the hospital and find out what this Swifty yegg knows."

Webbing put a file into the drawer. "No good, sir. They don't think he'll be up to an interview for a few days."

Burks strode toward the door. "I'll just take a ride down myself and see."

Burks pulled his sedan up to the entrance of the three story building. He found Swifty's room on the second floor by observing a young, slim uniformed officer outside it. The name on the officer's badge read 'Perkins.'

"How's he doin'?" Burks asked.

The officer looked up, his face a pale tinge of green. "Never looked better to me, Chief."

"Say," Burks rubbed his chin, "you're lookin' a little green around the gills. You okay?"

The officer nodded. "Things are looking up. Still, I need to use the lavatory. You don't mind taking over while I grab a rest and a coffee?"

Burks smiled. "Sure. I plan to be here a while."

"Truer words," Officer Perkins replied as he strode down the hall.

"What's that mean?" Burks asked as he placed his fingers on the door handle. He thought he heard the reply from the officer, but couldn't make it out. "Fresh punks," Burks muttered, pulling a cigar out of his pocket. He lit it with a silver lighter. "This city's police force is falling apart."

Burks opened the door to Swifty's room. The lights were out and the blinds were drawn, making it dark. He felt the wall for the light switch. Flipping it did nothing but make the sound of a click. Burks moved into the hall and shouted, "Hey, Fatman!" Not receiving a response he pulled his lighter and gun from his overcoat pocket.

Holding his gun in his right hand, he lit the lighter with his left and stepped into the room. The light flickered across the white walls and revealed Swifty's bandaged form, quite like a mummy as Webbing earlier attested. He moved over to the figure and felt the bandaged wrist. He moved quickly out of the room and kicked something light. It clattered across the floor. Holstering his gun, he followed it with the flickering flame-light. He bent over and picked up a syringe and pocketed it.

He rushed into the hallway looking for anyone. "Help!" he shouted. "Help! There's a murder in Room 216!"

"Don't be an idiot!" Burks shouted at Webbing as he pulled at the handcuffs around his wrists. "I didn't do it!" Behind his back his shaking fists opened and closed.

The uniformed officer shrugged. "I know that, sir. There's procedure, you know."

"To hell with procedure!" Burks said through gritted teeth. "We've got a crime to solve! You're arresting me while the green-faced man gets away! He's the killer, and probably X!"

Webbing nodded. "I am sorry, sir," he said. "The nurse saw you enter two hours ago."

"I just showed up half an hour ago!" Burks' face turned a unique shade of red. "Heck, I just saw you less than an hour ago at the police station! Come on man, you know I didn't kill this Carlos kid!"

Webbing cleared his throat. "I don't know sir...."

"Sure you do! You know the difference between right and wrong! You'll have to start taking the bull by the horns someday, rookie! Might as well start fresh!"

Webbing held up his hand to Burks and looked at the ceiling, deep in thought. Finally, he nodded. He took the key out of his pocket and removed the handcuffs. "Okay, Chief."

Burks calmly rubbed his wrists. "Good man, Webbing. Let's get after that green-faced man."

Webbing nodded and took the syringe out of his pocket. "I don't think we'll find any prints on this," he said. "Who do you think it could be?"

Burks laughed. "Are you kiddin' me? It was Agent X, of course!" He removed a fresh cigar and lit it. "This time, he's not getting away with it. Mark my words!"

Webbing gritted his teeth. "We'll get our man, sir."

The armored truck rolled down the street toward the Equity Bank. The sun beat the pavement until the heat rose from the blacktop in wavy streams. Pulling into the alley next to the bank, the truck rolled to a stop. The guards opened the doors while cautiously surveying the area. Tom Ellis alighted from behind the passenger's side bearing a pistol in his hands. "Looks clear, Lyle," he said.

The driver nodded. "Let's get this done before lunch and we'll stop by the bar."

Tom went to the back of the truck and put his keys in the lock. The door swung open and displayed white canvas bags with dollar signs on their sides. Placing his gun in his holster, Tom picked up a bag in each hand and pushed the door shut. The lock clicked as he turned to walk into the bank.

He looked up as the wind blew his hat off. A man with metal bird wings flew above him. He dropped one of the bags and pulled his gun too late. The gliding man swung about deftly and quickly, a machine gun in hand. The *ratta-tat-tat* noise spilled out as the bullets chewed the pavement. Tom danced under the volley and fell to the ground.

Lyle saw the winged man fire his gun, though he couldn't see his partner. "Tom!" he shouted as he opened the door to see the other guard lying in a pool of blood. Lyle swallowed the nausea as he grabbed his partner's arm to feel for a pulse. His head fell and he closed his eyes. "Tom…."

He heard the whooshing sound of wings. He looked up quickly to see the winged man returning. He pulled his gun and rushed back to the truck. He slammed the door as bullets hailed down, cracking the vehicle's bulletproof glass and pocking the armored sides. Lyle put the truck in gear and accelerated down the alleyway.

Swooping down like a bird of prey, the winged man followed the truck. Lyle could see the pursuer in his side mirror and slammed on the brakes. The truck spun 180 degrees as the tires squealed to a smoking halt. Bullets tore again at the sides of the truck as the winged man flew overhead. Lyle watched the flying attacker spin in the air to continue the pursuit. He sought maximum speed, the engine rumbling indecipherable invectives.

The winged pursuer quickly gained on the thundering vehicle. Lyle attempted to turn into a cross street, but the speed and angle proved inappropriate.

The axle snapped audibly, and the armored truck flipped onto its side and slid down the street on the passenger side. Lyle held onto the driver's wheel from pure instinct. The passenger side window shattered into nothingness under the strain. A ticker tape parade of sparks shot high into the air as the armor ground against the pavement.

The winged man flew by, still following his trajectory through the alley. The truck ground to a halt. Lyle released the steering wheel and landed against the passenger door in a state of semi-shock. Through the blood seeping into his eyes, he saw another winged man flying toward him before passing out.

The winged attacker flew back to the wrecked armored truck. He swooped toward the disabled vehicle just in time to see a man flying with a second winged contraption, obviously of the same manufacture. He glided upwards and brought his machine gun to bear as the second flyer approached. The other flyer already had a strange-looking gun aimed at the truck's attacker.

Before the first flyer could use his machine gun, he found himself flying into a cloud of greenish gas. The substance came from the nozzle of his flying adversary. He sucked in the gas in surprise. He coughed at the fumes, his eyes watering. The gas-cloud proved impenetrable to sight. Halfheartedly, he fired a wild round toward where he thought his foe might be. His eyes drooped as he dropped the Thompson from limp fingers. He felt strong arms grasp his armpits and carry him aloft as he slipped into unconsciousness.

Marty Glaves awoke with a headache on a concrete floor. He rubbed his sore arms, taking note that someone had removed the wing contraption. He rubbed his head and looked around the empty warehouse. Light filtered in through the high windows, mostly broken. A mouse scurried across the floor. It stopped to look at Marty curiously before rushing away.

Attempting to stand up, the gangster felt woozy and sat down. The warehouse door slid open, allowing a sliver of light and a man's slender figure to enter before shutting again.

"Who are you?" Marty asked as the man's shoes sounded in slow rhythm against the concrete.

No reply answered Marty's call. The figure kept moving toward him in easy, determined steps. The light slowly revealed the features of the man. He wore a tuxedo as if preparing for a nice dinner, yet his features made Marty gasp. Light-green skin described the bald face. The figure stared at Marty in silence as he took out a cigarette.

"Oh!" Marty said as he stood uneasily to his feet. "It's you, Fantômas." The man offered no reply, impelling Marty to elaborate. "I don't know what happened, but I'm pretty confident I killed the driver. That was what you said you wanted me to do."

If Marty hadn't seen the man walk in he might have thought it was a statue with a cigarette between its lips that stood in front of him. "Hey, look. I did as you asked. The other ravenman came and hit me, but I was done with my mission."

Almost imperceptibly, the statue shook its head, dislodging a spray of ashes and smoke. "You did not complete your mission," the green-faced man replied with the slight accent of a French aristocrat. "The driver is still alive and recuperating in the hospital."

Marty shook his head. "I don't know how that's possible."

"It is possible," Fantômas replied. "So very possible, it is true."

Marty looked up. "How did I get here, then?"

"I brought you here," Fantômas replied.

"You were the other ravenman?"

Fantômas nodded. "Of course. Who else has this technology? A glider is a simple contraption. Our improvements to the technology are groundbreaking." Fantômas replaced his cigarette with a fresh one and lit it with the remaining glow of its predecessor. "No one can stop my crimes now that I have Agent X where I want him. Miss Dale is under my power, which is the same as having X in my claws." Fantômas dropped the previous cigarette to roll across the concrete to ward Marty.

"Miss Dale? You mean the girl?"

Fantômas closed his eyes for a moment. "There is but one," he sighed. "X doesn't know where we are keeping her."

Marty smiled to be on the inside track. "It was pretty smart to make a space in the top floors of the unfinished Colodine Towers where we could launch. It's nearly invisible, and a perfect place to keep a captive. The construction's waiting until the company figures out how to kneed the dough it needs." Marty allowed a slight grin.

Fantômas removed his cigarette and examined it, twirling it slowly between his fingers. "It was pretty smart, Marty. I do not believe hiring you was wise, however."

Marty's face twisted in confusion. "What do you mean? I'm one of the best pilots of your contraptions!"

Fantômas smiled. "Don't you mean Fantômas' contraptions?" The cigarette between the green-faced man's fingers started to release green smoke. "As I said, I believe Fantômas trusts you, but you are not smart enough to keep quiet." X threw the used cigarette to the ground with the one releasing the green gas. They fell together and crossed into the shape of an 'X.'

"Ah, geez…" Marty coughed as he inhaled the gas.

"Don't worry, Marty," Secret Agent X said from his behind his green-faced guise. "Fantômas can't take revenge on you. I'll see you stay alive and incarcerated for a long, long time as a reward for the aid you've given me. I knew you would spill. You must not have spent enough time with

Fantômas to recognize his voice."

Marty fell to the ground unconscious, his legs folding under him. The cigarettes saved him from hitting his head too hard, though he would wake with another headache. Secret Agent X rolled him over to be sure he was unconscious and saw the 'X' imprinted on Marty's face in cigarette ashes. He peeled away his green mask as he walked out of the warehouse. "I'm coming for you, Fantômas," he murmured as he got into his car. He changed out of his disguise as he drove away.

Rubbing his glasses with a handkerchief, Professor Merrynk watched the headlights of a car pull into the driveway.

Cleaning the dishes from the kitchen table, his young niece walked to the window and looked over his shoulder. "Who is it, *mon oncle*?"

Merrynk shook his head lightly as he watched a figure of a man exit the sedan. He peered through the darkness, failing to discern the man's features. "I do not know, Vanessa. You should go to your room. I will meet this man alone."

After seeing that his niece left the room, Professor Merrynk walked to the door. He placed his hand on the doorknob just as a single, sharp rap announced the man. Merrynk breathed a silent sigh as he opened the door. "Hello? May I help you?"

Stepping back from the square-jawed man, Professor Merrynk examined the new arrival. The young fellow bore a physique of a college football player. His green fedora sported a black band. The band complimented his black suit if the hat did not. "I am looking for one Professor Merrynk."

The professor nodded. "I am he."

The man smiled reassuringly as he displayed a shiny badge to the professor. "Professor Merrynk, I am Operative number forty-eight Dunn. Though I work in a different agency, I am aiding Secret Agent X on an assignment. As his trusted friend, he asked me to interview you about information you might have."

Professor Merrynk nodded his grey head slowly. "I will help X in any way I can, Agent Dunn."

Taking off his hat, Dunn walked into the craftsman's home. "Thank you, Professor. I won't take much of your time." Merrynk cringed as the agent's hand disappeared into his jacket. He smiled as the agent produced a small piece of metal. "I apologize, Professor. I did not mean to frighten you. Agent X would have come to talk to you himself if he were not enmeshed in this matter."

Merrynk laughed. "I am jittery, my friend, that is all!" He grasped the piece of metal, weighing it in his hand. "It is incredibly light!"

Dunn nodded. "Yes, and strong to boot. Agent X needs to know what kind of metal it is. If possible, he needs to know how to fight someone who uses weapons made of this."

Merrynk ran his hand through his long, white hair. "I am a professor of psychology, Agent Dunn. I am familiar with metallurgy, though I am no expert by any stretch of the imagination. Why would Agent X come to me on this matter?"

Dunn shrugged. "He seems to trust your expertise more than you do."

The professor nodded. "I suppose I am more an admirer of precious metals rather than an expert. However, let me see what I can do."

Merrynk led Operative 48 into a laboratory with several vials along shelves on the wall. He placed the piece the agent handed him earlier under a microscope. "Interesting."

"What is it professor?" Dan asked.

Taking off his round-rimmed bifocals, Merrynk replied, "It appears to be a type of titanium alloy. I do not know what comprises the alloy aside from titanium in so short a time. The alloy is extremely light, although it would most assuredly be expensive and difficult to synthesize. It may take a month to discover its properties."

Tipping his hat back on his head, the secret operative let out a low whistle. "You can't help Agent X then."

"I did not say that," Merryk stated. "I do not need to know the properties of the metal. I believe I have something that will prove effective."

Walking over to one of the long shelves, Merrynk pulled a small, glass vial down. The opaque glass obscured its contents. "Here, Agent Dunn. This should be sufficient."

"What is it?"

"Are you familiar," the professor started, "with the manners of construction employed by the workmen on King Solomon's Temple?"

"Well, I know a bit about it," Dunn replied.

"Then you might be aware that the workmen used only tools of wood for building. Lesser known is that Insect Shermah rose from the desert to polish the stones while the workmen slept."

The agent nodded. "Okay. How does this help?"

Reaching behind a shelf of vials, Professor Merrynk produced a scroll.

He grasped the piece of metal, weighing it in his hand. "It is incredibly light!"

"Give this to Agent X, and relay to him what I have told you. It should be sufficient."

Dunn slipped the scroll and vial into the pockets of his overcoat and nodded. "Consider it done, Professor. Have a good night." With that, Operative 48 strode out of the laboratory.

Twilight moved between the skyscrapers, the stretching towers of Babel all racing to have the first conversation with the almighty. A fence surrounded the site, its metal already rusting from the hard weather. Paper and garbage pressed against the chain link, unconsciously constructing its own structure.

The green Hudson Terraplane was parked next to the construction site. The oddly-monikered car seemed somehow appropriate for hunting birds. Or ravenmen.

No time for further subterfuge, X opened the car door. Under his long trenchcoat, he still wore the guise of Fantômas. He rubbed his green chin in thought as he surveyed the area. The dust of the ground kicked up as a breeze whistled through the streets. X had met with Operative 48 the previous night, spending the early morning hours in preparation.

X looked up. Twenty stories looked complete. New windows awaited decorative curtains. The manner of construction seemed odd. The windows and walls normally waited for completion of the main structure. X merely shrugged. The naked iron girders stretched further into the air above the completed floors, hard fingers seemed to seek to grasp birds out of the air. A system of cylindrical tubes, probably the exposed veins of the air-handling system, entangled the iron girders. X gave up his musings, finding too many coincidental visuals to the current situation. He had to concentrate on saving Betty.

He walked up to the site's fence and deftly picked the padlock. He stepped inside, hearing a whistling sound. He pulled his forty-five and rushed behind a pile of iron girders as the machine gun played a cacophonous symphony off the metal. X waited as the glider flew overhead and fired a single shot at the flier.

A loud *ping* preceded the sound of metal snapping, and one of the gliderman's wings folded like a broken umbrella. Spinning onto his back, the gliderman flew uncontrollably as he fired his machine gun. Out of control and wild, the bullets carried the same promise of death as before.

X rushed to safety around the girders. The end of the hail of machine-gun bullets came with the punctuating sound of the gliderman crashing against the fence. X looked out to see the erstwhile flier crumpled against the fence and unconscious, a twisted parody of a raven.

X rushed over to the man, kicking away the discarded Thompson as he approached. He knelt next to the man and grasped his wrist. Though unconscious, battered and bruised, it seemed the gliderman would survive. X laid the man on the ground and covered him with his unbroken wing.

X scanned the ever-darkening sky for more glidermen, yet the night maintained mute silence. He stood and walked toward the building. Clearly, his presence was announced. He could not rely on subterfuge.

He walked to the large, ornate doors leading to the structure's lobby. He found them unlocked. He moved into the spacious room. Tall pillars of gray marble sent long shadows across the finished floors.

His steps resounded throughout the building as he walked toward the staircase, knowing the elevator operators were not on duty. Even if power ran to the elevators, the small boxes of convenience could become coffins should an enemy so choose.

Secret Agent X moved unmolested up the wide stairs and down the echoing hallways, cautiously searching each door he passed for possible threats.

He progressed uninhibited as he made it past floor after floor. Moonlight drifted in through the windows. The structure remained silent as a tomb. X knew that a trap awaited him, so he was prepared for it when a pair of men in suits appeared at the top of the stairs with machine guns and opened fire. Windows rattled under the reverberations as X leapt out of the way and into an adjoining hallway. Fully aware he was being herded by the gunsels, X had mere moments before they made their way down the stairway.

When the toughs arrived on the floor below, X was not in the hallway. They stepped cautiously down the darkened passage, checking the doors as they walked along. All the doors were locked, until they came across a doorknob that turned. The leading gunman put his fingers to his lips and gestured to his partner. The partner opened fire at the moment the leader thrust the door open. The door behind the two opened and the hallway filled with a cloud of green gas. The men fell to the floor coughing, their hats rolling off their heads as they fell into unconsciousness. X stepped out of the doorway and picked up the silent Thompsons. Removing a pen from his pocket, he wrote an 'X' on the cheeks of both men in red ink. He carried the machine guns with him and continued.

As he returned to the stairwell he met with a figure on the top of the stairs. A man dressed in a tuxedo, spats, and a top hat. He took a drag off the cigarette in its holder and laughed at X. "I am pleased you accepted my invitation, X. You have proved so very predictable."

"You mean," X replied, "you wanted me to interrogate your henchman. On the contrary, you are the predictable one, Fantômas. Your henchman was far too open with the information to actually have anything you wanted kept secret. Assuming you truly are as brilliant as the reputation that precedes you. You are proving far too transparent." X laughed. "You could just as easily have met me at a restaurant."

Fantômas tapped ashes off his cigarette and stretched the white gloves he wore tight over his slender, arachnid fingers. He smiled lightly. "Mister X, I hope you do not think me so common as to make an attempt at maintaining constant obscurity. Certainly, in my younger years, I reveled in my genius. Now that I approach the twilight of life, I find myself at a place where I desire a lesser obscurity. Valentino's a celebrity, and Hitler is a madman. They are household words in more countries than have a common language." He smiled broadly and lowered his chin, his eyes peering wryly out from beneath the brim of his hat. "I can do better. I will do better. I," he brought his hands to point inward at his chest, "I have done better, my friend."

X nodded and feigned a bored yawn. "You kidnapped a girl and deftly avoided buying me a cup of Joe at the corner diner. Yes, Fantômas. Your sinister genius fades with the years."

Fantômas started for a moment at X before letting a laugh reverberate throughout the tower. He clapped his hands in applause. "Bravo. Bravo! You know, of course, why I come to you, my dear X. I have heard your exploits rival my own in genius. You and I are destined to challenge each other." Fantômas blew a cloud of smoke. "I have arranged to have that challenge on my terms. When it is accomplished, the world will know each of us. They will know me as their leader. They will know you by your gravestone."

X brought the pair of Thompsons to bear on Fantômas. "You will release Miss Dale and we will finish this now."

Fantômas smiled. "I disagree with you, X. Let us not make a habit of such inconsistencies. Miss Dale is still in my power. If you wish to see her again, you will be more patient." Fantômas moved into the shadows. "We will conclude our confrontation soon, X. I am certain it has been your pleasure to meet me at last."

X gritted his teeth and fired a round into the empty darkness, knowing Fantômas was no longer there.

X continued the climb up the staircase until coming upon a metal set of double doors, decidedly separating the finished structure with the unfinished portions above. Carefully checking around the doorframe, he found no discernable rigging on the visible side of the door. Despite his presence here as Fantômas' apparent guest, he would assume nothing concerning the plans and motivations of the criminal genius. Fantômas had concocted some sinister plan for world domination, a plan he wished Secret Agent X to attempt to foil. Likewise, the master criminal assumed a triumph over X in the agent's attempt. X considered these matters, allowing the heavy overcoat he wore to fall away as he climbed the stairs.

Betty Dale awoke in a room meant to accommodate a prisoner. This startled her before she recalled the incident with the milkman. She examined herself, seeing that she wore her robe and nightgown, and appeared none-the-less for the wear. She sighed. *No need to panic,* she thought. No injury had come to her—yet. Fantômas must have needed her in good health as a bargaining chip against Agent X. She tightened her jaw to steel herself against the tortures she imagined Fantômas might subject her. His genius equaled his ruthlessness if the case studies from his operations in France held true.

Sitting up, Betty smoothed her robe and nightgown. She pulled her curly blonde hair out of her blue eyes. She examined the enclosure, about six feet by eight in her estimation. Riveted steel composed its stark, gray walls. The door, made of the same material, rigidly denied Betty's attempts to open it. The bed where she'd awakened proved simple yet sufficient with its single mattress and military blanket. A lightbulb hung by a cord from the ceiling above the bed. In one corner rested a rudimentary toilet, the only decoration in the entire room aside from the bed and light bulb.

Calmly, Betty listened for clues outside her confines. She heard the dim sound of wind brushing past the metal wall opposite the door. She nodded with the knowledge that one wall at least was an outside wall of whatever structure contained her prison. She walked to the metal toilet, examining it closely. Water rested in its basin. The separate tank rested on the wall above it, with a pull-chain for flushing. Obviously not of the latest design, yet it appeared new.

She returned to the door and examined the lock. It was heavy and utilitarian. Placing her hands on her hips, she looked at the light bulb hanging from the ceiling. She reached up and grabbed the electric cord. Tugging on it cautiously caused the cord to break the plaster, exposing more of the electrical wires hidden beneath. Nails holding the cord in place came down with it. The plaster coated the bed, yet Betty paid no attention. She pulled the light bulb and its cord until it hung dangling over the concrete floor.

Formulating a plan, she sighed. It was too easy, but she couldn't pass the opportunity. She removed her bathrobe and began tearing it into strips. She looked at the barred window and laughed as she continued her plans for the terrycloth.

Her robe now in long strips, she began to tie the strips together. Wearing only her nightgown, she shivered against the chill air. She carefully bundled the strips into a ball. Walking to the toilet, she dunked the ball into the water, soaking the remains of her robe. She pulled out the ball, stepping back from the cold water that ran over her shins. Tying a wet strip firmly to the door, she unraveled the ball. Taking the other end of the ball to the light bulb, she carefully tied it around the cord.

She returned to the bed and took off the thick blanket. This, she took to the toilet and soaked as she had the roll of terrycloth strips. It was more difficult to soak entirely, yet she managed. It dripped all over the concrete floor as she carried it over to place it in front of the door.

Looking around the room, Betty returned to the toilet. She put the seat down and stood on the lid. She then screamed as loudly as she could. She went silent again and listened. Heavy boots reverberated as they ran toward the door. They got louder. Betty sighed as she decided there was only one pair of boots. That meant there was only one guard coming. She allowed a smirk as she thought it could be two guards, each hopping on one leg. She discarded her mental frivolity and watched the door intently. She screamed once more, and the boots ran faster.

Watching the door intently, she heard some keys jangle, followed by the sound of a key sliding into the lock. Betty breathed deeply as someone pulled the door open. A man wearing a black mask with goggles and matching wing contraption rushed in. He looked around, confused at the disarray of the room. The wet terrycloth jerked at the door being opened, and the electric cord and light bulb crashed to the floor. Betty gasped as the light bulb bounced on the soaked blanket but didn't break.

The winged man laughed as he walked toward the light bulb. "That was dumb, ya dizzy dame!"

Betty's mind raced. She smiled, and then started laughing. "Yeah, I guess it was pretty silly!"

Picking up the light bulb, the man looked up to see Betty in her nightgown. She used all her feminine wiles as she looked at him. "Since I'm not getting out of here, I guess you've got me all to yourself."

As the winged man moved excitedly forward, Betty kicked his hand with bone-crunching force. The light bulb fell to the ground and smashed. The man twisted as the electricity flowed through the soaked blanket. He fell to the floor, still writhing under the effects of the electricity. With the bulb broken, the man's lightning-enshrouded body provided the only light in the room. He'd become a human lightbulb!

Betty's eyes widened in horror when she realized the man might die. She didn't want to kill him, only disable him so she could escape! She resisted the urge to rush over and grab him. She began thinking how to disable the electricity.

Looking around the room offered nothing Betty could use. She looked at her feet, realizing the lid of the toilet tank might help. She lifted the heavy ceramic lid and tossed it, discus-style, at the cord on the bed. The heavy piece landed on the cord and bounced it into the air. Betty moved quickly as the light went out. She jumped onto the bed and grabbed the falling live wire. She deftly caught it with the broken bulb suspended in the air. She held the cord at arm's length, careful to not let it come back and electrocute her. She stepped off the bed onto the floor and dropped the wire onto the mattress.

Making her way across the wet floor, she came to the man's side. The light from the open door allowed her to examine him. She sighed in relief as she realized he was still breathing. She took his pulse, deciding it seemed good. Her knees in the cold water caused her to shiver. She removed the gloves from the man's hands and put them on. They made her feel warmer and gave her an idea.

In about three minutes, the unconscious man had been stripped of his bird's wings. Betty looked down in the dim light, pleased at how well the suit fit her. It was disappointing, she thought, that it accented her gender too much. She liked the look, but if she had to use it as a disguise the outfit would not stand up to close scrutiny. Betty shrugged her shoulders before placing the black mask, actually a helmet of strong, thin metal covered with leather, over her head.

The wings proved quite light and did not greatly obstruct Betty's movements. Picking up the ravenman's Tommy gun, she strode confidently out the door. She shut and locked it behind her. She looked down the concrete hallway. It ended to the right and the corridor continued to the left. She walked past the doors and empty frames where work had ceased. She could not contemplate the hallway long, as another ravenman turned the corner ahead and rushed toward her. She breathed in, but remained calm.

"Joe!" the other ravenman shouted. A hint of excitement tinged his voice. "Joe, we've got to get ready for the attack! It's starting!"

The ravenman grabbed Betty's arm and pulled her along, not noticing her figure. She almost felt insulted as she ran. The man was too excited to notice much. Betty had no choice for the moment. She followed the rushing ravenman.

They ran down the corridor, which opened into an enormous room with ceilings 50-feet high. Several ravenmen flew in the air above their heads. Across the room stood a grouping of ravenmen waiting on a ledge in the room where no wall stood. Lit only by moonlight, the scene caused Betty to gasp. The ravenman pulling her took no notice as he released her arm and rushed toward the precipice. "Come on, Joe!"

Betty did not wish to follow, but ten ravenmen came from behind them at a running pace. Betty would bring unwanted notice to herself if she did not follow. She watched as the ravenmen spread their wings and stepped, straight-legged, off the floor and fell out of sight. Betty slowed to see how the others took flight by manipulating the wings. She mimicked their motions, bringing her wings outward. A passing ravenman startled her as he struck her shoulder hard as he ran by. He stopped and turned around. "Why are you wet?"

Betty rushed toward the yawning maw of darkness. She deepened her voice and said, "I took a birdbath."

"That's funny Joe—you're a laugh riot!" The ravenman turned and kept running as he shouted back, "Come on, Joe, get with it! It's now or never!"

Beneath the mask, Betty nodded and mumbled, "It's now or nevermore." Betty ran after the ravenman and watched him plunge into the dark night. She came to the precipice and closed her eyes.

Waking in his shorts and socks, Secret Agent X sat up on the wet blanket. He chuckled and shook his head. If he'd revealed his disguise to Betty none of this would have happened. He stood up and looked around. He could see very little in the darkness: the only illumination came from the bottom of the door. That sparse light and his training allowed him to see the scant contents of the room. He sighed as he tore a deep gash into his throat. Blood dripped from the wound as he calmly dug beneath the skin and retrieved a thin, metal lockpick.

Licking the artificial blood off the pick, X placed it in the lock. With incredible celerity, he quickly disabled the lock.

The light flooded the room as he pushed the door open. He looked down the hallway and saw a ravenman walking toward him.

"Help!" he shouted, clutching his bleeding neck. "It's me, Joe!"

The ravenman rushed toward him. "Joe!? What happened?"

X slumped against the wall and slid to the floor, shaking his head. "She cut my throat," he said weakly.

The ravenman set his Thompson machine gun on the floor and knelt next to X to look at the wound. "Cripes, Joe, don't move! It looks bad!"

Feigning his injury until the ravenman neared, X pushed the ravenman hard against the wall and grasped the ravenman's Thompson with a lightning-quick motion. The gun pointed at the ravenman's head. "Hands on your head!" X barked. "Get into the room!"

Following the ravenman into the room, X ordered, "Take off your uniform and give it to me!"

Reluctantly, the ravenman stripped off his flying outfit. He handed pieces of the uniform to Secret Agent X. "Move over to the far wall and lay down!" X ordered the nearly naked man. X promptly donned the outfit. He threw a vial of liquid against the far wall, which broke open. Gas spewed from the broken vial, putting the erstwhile ravenman to sleep. In the full, winged uniform, X walked out, locking the door behind him. X rushed down the hallway.

It took him moments to traverse the hallway. Ravenmen rushed toward the edge of the enormous floor and into the night air. Scanning the crowd of dark, winged forms, X noted a female figure beneath one of the uniforms. He stifled a shout as he saw Betty move toward the edge and fall off. He ran forward and leapt into the night air.

His eyes adjusted to the light, and the glass in his helmet eyepieces helped him see in the darkness. Flying around haphazardly like bees around a hive, the ravenmen formed into cohesive and uniform groups.

The secret agent began to move toward Betty Dale in his uniform that she'd usurped from him earlier. She obviously did not have a hang of the wing-apparatus, yet she discovered quickly how to make it fly. He glided next to her. Using a voice that only Betty would recognize was his, he said, "How are you doing, Joe?"

Betty turned her head to look into the masked features of Secret Agent X. "It's you!" she whispered harshly.

X nodded. "We must follow the leader for now. The scenario will unfold as we go along."

Betty pulled on the strap of her Thompson. "Why do they use these? They are very impractical when flying."

X nodded. "That's true. The mind of Fantômas is difficult to understand."

Betty snorted. "Not to me. He's just an egotistical, maniacal, criminal genius."

"That's quite a mouthful, Betty." X looked at the other ravenmen flying with them. "You're not getting paid to write right now. Save the nickel words and follow me!" X headed to join the formation.

"Yeah," Betty mumbled as she watched X fly away. "I'm doing this because I'm getting paid, and not because I'm hopelessly in love with you, X." She sighed and breathed deep. Twisting in the air, Betty followed the enigmatic X into formation with the rest of the ravenmen.

The long line of ravenmen flew toward the bay. Light from the full moon shimmered off the surface of the water. Betty came next to Agent X toward the end of the line. "Where do you suppose we're going?" she asked in a whisper.

"I'd guess the mission is in the bay," X suggested. "Perhaps Fantômas wants to destroy a ship."

"It seems anti-climactic," Betty said. "Building an army of flying men to destroy a ship?"

X shrugged. "It's likely bigger than that. It's always best to start with the simplest guess. We'll have to ride this out to catch the game."

"I don't think it'll take very long," Betty replied and pointed her finger into the darkened bay. "Look!"

Secret Agent X followed the imaginary line made by Betty's black gloved hand. He struggled to speak before blurting out, "Impossible!"

They both looked on at the black battleship far out in the harbor, nearly invisible in the darkness. With guns jutting like pins in a pincushion, the ship was loaded for bear. It pulled next to an American battleship. Betty cleared her throat. "How did that get past the Navy?"

"I don't know," X admitted. "We have to stop it! The Navy won't be able to handle that monstrosity by themselves, and there aren't any other ships here!"

"That's where the ravenmen are headed," Betty said, "but I don't understand why?"

"To act as escorts for the ship," X replied. "The ravenmen will clear all opposition. If the ship attacks the city, thousands will die tonight!"

"Get the squad car, Webbing!" Burks shouted as he stomped into police headquarters.

Webbing stood, pulling on his jacket as he headed for the door. "What's the rush, Burks?"

"One of them chicken hawks is lying dead in the district," Burks replied between chomping on his cigar. "He must have fallen out of his cage is all I can figure."

Webbing held the door for Burks, who stormed through it in a sparking cloud of ash and smoke. "Hurry up, kid. You'll be at my funeral before we get there at the rate you're moving!"

The rookie sighed and followed Burks into the haze of cigar smoke. "Hey, Burks, don't you know smoking will kill you?"

Burks continued walking. "I know I'll kill you if you try to nursemaid me again, punk!"

Webbing chuckled under his breath as he got into the driver's seat. "Okay, Burks. Don't get worked up. Your heart probably can't take the stress."

"Just drive, Rookie," Burks grumbled as he got in the car. "We need to carve up this turkey and figure out who cooked its goose and why."

Burks whistled as they pulled into the yard of the Colodine Towers. Ravenmen poured forth in steady streams toward the bay. Burks pulled his revolver. "Get your gun, Webbing! Don't know what these magpie jokers are up to, but I can tell they stacked the deck!"

Two Ravenmen saw the policemen and flew toward them. Burks fired as they drew near while Webbing took cover behind the car. "What are you doin', Rookie? It ain't a talkie, these guys are serious!"

Webbing nodded and pointed at the ravenmen. "Get your head down Burks! Those guys have machine guns!"

One of the ravenmen opened fire. Bullets began to pock the ground. Burks leapt behind the squad car. "I'm gettin' too old for this stuff, Rookie!

Outrunning machine guns is a young man's game."

Webbing looked over the hood of the car. "Yeah? I don't like this game anymore than you do. Want to turn the table?"

"Dang, kiddie," Burks chewed his cigar. "If you've got a way to make a play, you pitch and I'll catch!"

"Okay." Webbing replied. "I'm gonna play Cy Young. Hold your breath for a minute!"

"What?"

Webbing replied by standing up and throwing a sphere the size of a baseball. It struck the nearest ravenman, exploding into a cloud of green gas. The ravenman dropped his machine gun and fell from his place ten yards up.

"Nice arm, kid! You took it home! Where the heck did you get the fancy baseball? I didn't see you carrying it!"

Webbing shrugged, remembering the package delivered to his home. A simple note said, "These will work. X."

"It was sent to me this morning by a secret admirer. The note said that Fantômas is behind the ravenmen."

"Who's this Fantômas character? Like Karloff?"

"I think more like Phantom of the Opera, but I don't know a lot about him."

The other ravenman opened fire on the car. "Since you're not a speakeasy, I'm not gonna ask where you got the snazzy snowglobe, but you got any more?"

Webbing shook his head. "Just that one." The rookie swallowed, glad that Burks didn't press the question. It would complicate matters if Burks knew Webbing was actually Gerald Dake, an agent of X, disguised as Webbing. Burks looked up at the other ravenmen diving toward them. Burks and Webbing retreated behind the squad car again. "Didn't your teacher tell you to bring enough treats for everyone?"

"Sure—but nobody told me how many were coming to the Valentine's party. I'm all out of that flavor." Webbing smiled.

"You mean you brought cookies, too?"

Webbing nodded. "With milk to dip 'em in." To illustrate, Webbing made his way over to the trunk and reached for the handle. He retreated as a burst of bullets struck the trunk. The trunk popped open as the ravenman flew away. Turning to make another pass, the ravenman pinpointed Webbing. Webbing reached into the cardboard box delivered to him earlier in the day. He retrieved another glass sphere. He rolled his shoulders to clear them and turned to the ravenman just as the latter was some thirty yards away. Webbing spun his arm and released the sphere. It flew toward the ravenman just as the flyer pulled the trigger.

The ravenmen dived toward the American battleship and opened fire with their Thompson machine guns. As sailors in black uniforms rushed about the deck, the ravenmen mowed them down in a hail of bullets.

Secret Agent X clenched his teeth. "They are attacking that ship!" He dived toward the ship and ran into a ravenman. The surprised ravenman swung his machine gun around, but X knocked it out of the man's hands. He swung his fist at the flying man, connecting with the softer leather covering the man's abdomen rather than the steel-hard mask. Midair, the man doubled over and went into a head-over-heels spin.

X took one of the man's wings in his fist and tore it off. The man plummeted toward the stygian waters below.

Betty flew next to X. "One down, and all the rest to go! What do we do now?"

X looked at the attacked ship. Sailors with rifles took cover on the deck as the ship's lights swept the sky. Behind heavy metal plates, they fired shots into the swarm of gadflying ravenmen. A wild bullet came near his head. The ship shook as a shell exploded on its starboard side. "The black ship is attacking! I may not be able to stop it myself! You stay back Betty. It's dangerous."

"When is it not dangerous around you?" she retorted. "I want to stay and help!"

Shaking his head, X plummeted again. "I'm ordering you to leave! I can't afford the concern for your safety! I have to get on Fantômas' ship!"

Betty turned to fly away. "I'm leaving, X," she murmured. "We're going to talk about this when it's all over!" She stopped and turned in the air. "To hell with that! I'm not just some frail, X! I'm coming too!" Biting her lip, she flew with resolve after X.

Ravenmen began to coat the attacked ship. The sailors fought valiantly, yet the ravenmen gathered the upper hand. The other ship fired its cannon again. The blast threw sailors into the air. X went directly for Fantômas' ship. He landed on the deck without incident. In the confusion he walked safely on deck among the agents of Fantômas wearing dark sailor uniforms and the few ravenmen looking on. He observed as Fantômas' sailors came and went on the deck from below the ship. He casually went into the ship.

One of Fantômas' agents dressed as a sailor stopped him. "Why are you down here?" the man demanded. "Only injured ravenmen are allowed!"

"I have to get to the engine room," X replied instantly. "I saw a fuel leak."

The agent turned and waved his hand over his shoulder. "It's this way."

Secret Agent X couldn't believe his luck. Once out of sight, he cold-cocked the agent with the butt of his Thompson. He opened a door and pulled the limp form quickly out of the hallway into a storage room.

Shutting the door behind him, he quickly stripped off the Ravenman's uniform and removed the clothes from the unconscious agent of Fantômas. Once into the newly acquired sailor uniform, he tied up and gagged the enemy agent and strode into the hallway, shutting the door behind him. He watched men down the corridor greet each other and offer a salute by placing both hands in front of their neck and pulling them across in a slashing motion. 'Fant' they said to each other in an apparent password. Walking down the corridor, X imitated the salute and salutation when appropriate.

A klaxon bell rang throughout the halls. Sailors rushed down the hallway on their way to duties. X joined the mad-but-organized rush. No one questioned him and no one took time to salute. Some of the sailors rushed up and down ladders and stairs of black metal. X decided to stay with the small grouping that continued down the hallway. At the end of the hallway, the secret agent saw they were headed for the control room. Lights flashed off the walls as they entered the control room. Enigmatically, the men at the ship's controls stood and left their chairs as the entering sailors took up the abandoned seats. The leaving sailors rushed off to other stations in the ship.

Secret Agent X continued to stand toward the back of the room until he was approached by the captain on the bridge. "What are you doing here, Caparov?" the Captain demanded of X. "You are not assigned to this area!"

X repeated the salute and password. The Captain looked at him and pulled his pistol. "You are not Caparov! Seize him!"

The secret agent did not lose a moment. His hand rushed forward in one quick movement to grab the pistol from the captain's hand as his right arm turned around the Captain to clench his neck in a vice grip. Secret Agent X dug the pistol into the captain's back. The sailors stood quickly and drew their pistols. "Stop!" X ordered. "Stop, or I will shoot your Captain!"

The ship jerked suddenly. X lost his footing as it tipped impossibly backward, yet he held onto the Captain. Both men fell to the floor, the Captain on top of Secret Agent X, the latter releasing a *whoof* as his lungs compressed. He gripped the pistol tighter.

The Captain struck his left elbow into the secret agent's ribs. X out of breath already, it didn't impact him more. He struck the Captain with the butt of the pistol and pulled the unconscious man to his feet. "I will shoot him unless you do as I say!"

X felt the air move behind him. He spun around just as a large sailor swung his powerful fist. The fist slammed into X, throwing him and his unconscious captive hard against the wall. X turned the pistol on the bearlike sailor, but the massive man's arm caught X's hand in a vice grip. The secret agent gritted his teeth as his hand was slammed against the wall. X held onto the gun, but the sailor slammed it again into the wall with a roar. The telltale cracking sound in his hand accompanied great pain. X dropped the gun from his broken hand. X dropped the Captain to swing his left hand at the man's jaw, connecting with a resounding crunch. X's wrists were grasped from behind as he felt a sharp blow to the back of his head. Falling unconscious, he felt no more.

The throbbing pain in his skull forced Secret Agent X into consciousness. Blood dripped from his eyelids as he immediately attempted to assess the situation. He could see it was dark, as opposed to being blinded from the blow he recalled receiving. He was outside, judging from the cool, sea-salt laden breeze that teased the thick fog. Two men grasped each of his arms around his elbows. He could not see them, yet knew they were male and strong by the way they held his arms. Sounds of surf and buoy bells indicated the closeness of the shore. He lifted his head.

"Greetings, Secret Agent X," a voice said. Raising his head, X looked at the black-clad man with a greenish hue to his bald head. The figure stood ten feet away on the bow of the ship.

"Fantômas!" X seethed through his gritted teeth.

Fantômas nodded, displaying white teeth in a sardonic grin. "It is good to meet you again, X. But obviously not for you."

"Whatever your plan, Fantômas," X stated, "you will fail. You've waited too long."

Fantômas laughed. "You suppose yourself equal to me? You suppose you are my nemesis? I have no equal, and you are at a disadvantage."

Secret Agent X offered an easy smile. "I'm best when I'm at a disadvantage."

"Fantômas!" X *seethed through his gritted teeth.*

Fantômas lowered his eyelids. "As I am when my foe is at a disadvantage. I never show mercy. I make swift and final actions."

X smiled broadly. "As do I." X said, tensing his muscles. His body leaned forward quickly and with great force. The men holding the secret agent's arms suddenly found themselves thrown through the air.

X quickly noted that the men holding him wore sailor uniforms. He followed their progression, punching one in the kidney as the man was still mid-air. The sailor crashed to the deck, bent over in pain, as his cohort pushed himself up on his knees. X leapt at him, his leg foremost. His leather boot struck the man on the jaw with a *crack*. Blood and teeth ejected into the air as the sailor's head struck the deck.

X leapt to lay flat behind the body as a gunshot shook the chilled fog. The bullet struck the prostrate sailor in the chest. Blood spattered across his face as the bullet tore through the man, a soft whisper of breath blowing over X from the sailor's punctured wound.

From his vantage point, X saw the other sailor attempt to stand. The man held his side as he wheezed from the kidney punch the secret agent delivered some moments ago. X heard the sound of pressure applied to the gun trigger float on the cool air. The agent tore the pistol from the sailor's holster before rushing toward the other man as another bullet struck the sailor he'd hid behind a millisecond before.

Another bullet tore the deck as Fantômas moved to strike the agent. X plowed into the other sailor with a blow to the man's chin. He spun to aim his newly discovered pistol at Fantômas. The green-faced man prepared to fire as Secret Agent X brought his pistol to bear.

A strafe of machine gun bullets from above splintered the deck, causing Fantômas to leap to the side. X used the respite to steal a glance at the Thompson's operator and smiled. It was Betty Dale in her Ravenman disguise, flying gracefully over the deck, firing the machine gun. X turned his gaze to Fantômas and rushed at his foe.

As Betty spun in the air to take another run at Fantômas, the mastermind rushed forward to greet the secret agent. X struck the first blow, pushing the green face to the side. Fantômas replied with a punch to X's stomach, though the agent was prepared. The blow was ineffectual against the tensed muscles of the secret agent's abdomen.

X heard a whooshing sound behind him. He leapt out of the way as the *click* of a Thompson's trigger reached his ears. He rolled to the black metal of the bow, looking up at the figure firing the Thompson. It was Betty again, firing vehemently at Fantômas. To his guilt, X had opportunity to see the woman he loved in a state of undress, and his photographic mind imprinted her lovely figure indelibly in his mind.

The bullets from the Thompson ripped into the deck once more. Ricocheting bullets and splintering wood flew through the air all around Fantômas as the green-faced man laughed with mad hilarity. Fantômas retrieved a pistol from his black jacket to fire a single shot.

X's heart jumped as the bullet bounced off Betty's helmet. She plunged to the deck and slid across it with the machine gun released from her unconscious form. X bit his lip to keep from crying her name aloud. The machine gun slid toward him. He leapt to grasp it. Fantômas fired at the secret agent. The bullet hit X in the chest. With pain shooting through him, X ignored it and brought the Thompson to bear. "Give it up, Fantômas! Betty couldn't hit you because you hypnotized her to not hit you! I have no such compunction, and your pea-shooter is outclassed!"

Fantômas laughed. "Is it, X? Try firing it!"

X heard a click inside the Thompson and threw it to the deck. "Radio controlled safety on all the guns? Not bad, Fantômas."

Fantômas nodded agreement. "It is ingenious, X, as is this conspiracy I have here contrived." He waved his left arm about while keeping the pistol trained on X. "You do know that I was retired, don't you? Common crime so bored me." He shook his head. "It proved fun initially, yet outsmarting the world's law enforcement is too simple. I am too close to death. Cancer riddles my body. All the genius in the world, including mine, cannot save my ravaged corpse of a body. I have been outwitted by no man. Only fate will fell me. This ship, with the ravenmen, will continue to Washington. No cannons or aeroplanes can stop it. The weapons of man are too weak. They cannot stand against me."

Fantômas coughed before continuing. "I want to be remembered, X. I am certainly the greatest criminal the world has ever known. I want the whole world cowering at my feet before I die."

X shrugged. "It's good to have goals."

Fantômas laughed. "You are using humor, X; do not think I fail to recognize your sarcastic attitude! For your paltry attempts to amuse everyone, I will keep you alive long enough to die this night with the rest who oppose me!"

Sailors rushed to the deck. Regaining consciousness, Betty stood and grabbed the Thompson, preparing to fire at the oncoming sailors. X shouted: "Betty! Don't!"

Betty paused at the order and turned to look quizzically at the secret agent.

X nodded. "Drop it. Trust me."

She shrugged, sending her Thompson clattering to the deck. She watched X as two sailors rushed up and grabbed her black-clad arms.

Other sailors rushed over to capture the secret agent. X glowered at them. "Do not touch me. I will go with you without violence." His voice lowered. "If you harm one hair on her head," he nodded toward Betty being led away, "nothing can protect you from my vengeance." X smiled and waved his hand toward Betty. "Lead on."

X watched as the sailors escorted Betty through the door and down the metal stairs. X followed them with the sailors escorting him trailing behind, aiming their pistols at his back.

Walking through the metal door, the secret agent descended the stairs. None of the sailors looked at his face, at his right eye. The face of X twisted in concentration as he forced the eye to pop out of its place. With a slight twist, the eye evacuated the socket entirely and fell against the metal stairs. The glass eye shattered and cracked open as X's real eye moved forward and replaced the false one in the socket. A greenish gas escaped the ocular sphere and filled the air. The sailors escorting him coughed violently. They dropped their guns to bring their hands to their necks. They stumbled and fell against the stairs unconscious.

X ignored his erstwhile captors and their discomfort as he leapt upon the sailors holding Betty's arms. He grasped the first around the neck as the other went for his holstered pistol. Gritting his teeth, he pressed the sailor in his grasp against the other and pushed them both into the wall. The pistol became pointed away from both men as X pressed his advantage. Still holding the first man about the neck, X kicked harshly at the wrist of the second sailor. The wrist gave way with a violent crack. Blood spurted forth as the gun clattered to the floor. X released the neck of the now unconscious sailor, moving forward in a pugilistic stance against the other. The sailor held his hand in pain and sank to his knees. "Please, I can't do anything to resist!"

X raised his fist. "True," he replied as he delivered a crushing blow against the sailor's head. "But you can raise an alarm. I can't afford that."

Betty turned to the secret agent. "Thanks, X!" She looked at his face. "Are you crying?"

Secret Agent X shook his head. "No," he said. "I had to use my false eye. It's not comfortable, yet most people won't check if you're hiding something in your eye socket."

Betty shuddered. "Ewww!"

X laughed. "I know it doesn't sound pleasant. It isn't, either. The surgery to allow for that ability proved complex and painful, yet I was broken up anyway."

"I don't want to know more," Betty said. "How do we stop this? It seems impossible!"

"Not if you take off that fancy pants suit you're wearing," the secret agent replied.

Betty crossed her arms over her chest and blushed. "That doesn't sound helpful!"

X nodded grimly. "I can assure you, it is, Miss Dale. This is no jest."

Betty hesitated. She looked into the secret agent's eyes for a moment until it became embarrassing. "Okay," she consented. She pointed to a door marked as a storage closet. "Can we go in there?"

X went to the door and tried it. It opened easily into a room full of linens. "Come on," he nodded. "This will work."

Betty followed X into the room. He shut the door behind them as she reluctantly began to undress. The secret agent turned his head to give her privacy. He cleared his throat. "I am truly sorry about this, Betty."

With a soft sigh, Betty replied, "You know how I feel about you. I wish this happened under marital circumstances." A tear teased the corner of her eye. "Here," she said, handing the leather shirt forward.

Without turning, X reached behind to grasp the leather material. Betty grasped his hand, holding it for a long moment. X closed his eyes. "Now is not the time, Betty."

She placed her hand on his shoulder and pressed her lips to his neck. "When? Don't you want this?"

X brusquely shrugged her away. "Of course, I want you, Betty! I want to deserve you, and I deserve nothing until Fantômas is stopped." The secret agent turned to look into her eyes. "You're still under Fantômas' hypnotic suggestion!"

Betty crossed her arms to cover her bra. "That's too easy for you, isn't it? It may be true but all I know is it feels real to me! You say it does for you!" Betty grasped X's shoulders, drawing him into a passionate kiss.

X allowed his shoulders to droop, returning the kiss. After a moment, he gently pushed her away. "I am sorry, Betty. Just know that I love you."

Betty's mouth opened to reply as the entire ship shook. X gritted his teeth. "They are firing cannons! It has to end now!" X knelt with Betty's relinquished ravenman costume. He began to tear the inner lining out in long strips.

Betty watched X. "What are you doing?"

"Getting the weapon I sewed into the lining," X replied. He stopped to look up at Betty. "You and I may not survive this weapon ourselves."

Betty nodded solemnly. "If we can't be together, dying together is a proper substitute."

The secret agent nodded his reply and returned to removing from the uniform a handful of tiny vials containing what seemed to be short, red maggots. The maggot-like creatures squirmed around. X held up one of the vials.

"They're disgusting!" Betty said.

X shrugged. "They are beautifully destructive to Fantômas' plans."

"They are just worms!" Betty protested.

"Not just worms," X shook his head. "Insect Shermah."

"They sure look like 'just worms.'" Betty's face turned white.

X laughed. "They're not so bad. They eat every kind of metal known to man."

"If they help, that's great. I think they're hideous looking."

"Just watch." X opened one of the vials. Betty retreated as he spilled the tiny worms onto the floor. The worms twisted around each other, squirming into a knot on the metal floor.

"They aren't doing anything," Betty said.

"They're just thinking," the secret agent replied, "Be patient. It won't take long."

True to the prediction made by X, the worms began to dig holes in the floor's metal surface.

"That's amazing!" Betty admitted. "When do they stop?"

"When they run out of food," X replied as he looked around. "It doesn't look like that will happen for a while. When they've eaten enough, they reproduce by breaking into two worms, each as ravenous as the first. That takes a lot of energy. They never stop eating until they run out of food and die."

In moments, the worms created a hole in the floor and were opening it wider as they moved across the room.

Betty gasped. "They'll have this entire ship eaten in no time!"

Secret Agent X opened the door. "It will take a little longer than that. We'd best leave this room or we'll soon have nothing to stand on."

Betty nodded as she followed the secret agent through the door. She thought for a minute before quickly grabbing a large blanket off a shelf and wrapping it over her body to cover her underclothes.

"We'll have to move quickly," X said. "Those worms will be all over the ship soon."

"You only set out one vial," Betty said. "You brought more. Why didn't you use them?"

The secret agent didn't reply as they rushed onto the deck. A ravenman flew over the ship toward them, his machine gun blazing.

Secret Agent X threw a vial of worms at the ravenman. The worms spread instantly over the uniform, shredding the metal armor beneath. In moments, they enmeshed the gun. Soon after, they devoured the ravenman's metal wings. The man plummeted to the deck. The distance of the fall rendered the man unconscious on impact.

"Wow," Betty said. "Those work fast!"

X nodded. "Yes, but when they are out of food, they just die. The worms can't fly either. They won't attack the ravenmen unless they are thrown at them. Hopefully, that vial I used already will strip those aboard of their wings and guns."

A voice behind them rang through the air. "You will wish you hadn't faced me, Agent X." X spun with Betty to face Fantômas.

The secret agent smirked beneath his mask. "I've faced worse, or better, depending on how you look at things."

Fantômas smiled, his green-skinned face stretching broadly. "I am both better, and worse, you will find."

X gritted his teeth and rushed forward to the attack. "We've already done this, Fantômas! Are you ready for more?"

Fantômas waited for X to arrive. "If I recall, we did not decide the contest."

X threw a punch at Fantômas. "Your fate is upon you. We'll decide it now, once and for all time!"

Gerald Dake, in his disguise as the Police rookie named Webbing, still reeled from the effects of throwing the glass sphere. He ducked away from the machine gun blasts the ravenman fired, yet still managed to see the fantastic effects delivered by the exploding sphere. The worms it contained he knew nothing about until they rushed over the ravenman and devoured first the gun, followed by the metal armor beneath the suit and finally the wings. The ravenman struck the ground hard.

"Good arm, rookie!" Burks shouted. "Is that all of them?"

Webbing nodded. "I sure hope so, lieutenant. My arm's liable to get sore if I have to keep pitching fastballs against machine guns. It's just been pure luck so far. Those winged fellahs really have the home field advantage in the air."

Burks nodded. "Well, I don't see any more plumage in the air for now. Maybe we got 'em all."

Webbing's eyes widened as he pointed above them. "Maybe we've just been tossing eggs in the chicken coop. Looks like the mother hen's come to roost!" The rookie pointed at the enormous ship that floated over them.

"Holee!" Burks exclaimed. "What the heck is that?"

The rookie shrugged. "Looks like a big flying battleship to me, sir."

"Don't get smart, Webbing. It doesn't look natural on you. Where did it come from?"

"I'm thinking the harbor," Webbing replied. "That's where boats usually come in. What do you think of the harbor?"

"I think the harbor's an awful cup of Joe laced like the drinks at a murder party. I think you're gettin' awful wise, punk, and I can put that smart mouth of yours to eatin' dirt if you don't can the corn you're spittin' out of it. That was a free example of proper police banter for you."

Looking up again, Webbing replied, "I think we ought to stop talking and figure out what can be done about that disastrous dirigible above us."

Burks looked up and nodded. "Leave the writing to the Vernes of the world, kid. I think we'd better try something, 'cause as far as I know, we are the cavalry."

"Why's it falling to pieces?"

Burks shrugged. "If you were right and it spent any time in that outhouse they call City Harbor, our drinking water's probably doing to it what it does to my liver."

"I think that's the alcohol, sir," Gerald replied with a sigh. He shrugged. "Let's start running up the steps."

Burks followed Gerald as they rushed toward the building. "Let's hope there's an elevator in operation. Alcohol or not, my liver can't take much more abuse."

The pair rushed into the building. Gerald ran over to an elevator and pulled the switch to call it. They heard the motors whir. "What do ya' know!" Burks said.

When the elevator arrived, Burks took the controls. "Ain't sayin' I don't trust you, rookie. This is my life too, and I'm gonna steer this cage." The lieutenant pushed the lever forward and the cage jerked into motion.

As the cage carried them past the darkened floors, Burks turned to Webbing. "You know, rookie, I ain't always the sharpest knife in the drawer, but I figure you're working for someone else here."

Gerald sighed. "I suppose it's only fair you know. I'm working for Agent X."

Burks clenched his jaw. "I knew that punk was behind this somehow!"

"What are you going to do with me now?"

Burks tapped the gun under his jacket. "I know what I should do with ya. What's X playing at here? Wanting to muscle Fantômas' racket, whatever the heck that is?"

Gerald shrugged. "I don't know. I know we're doing a good thing here. That's all that matters."

"Okay, Don Quixote. X has played against the law too long."

"You've got a beef with X. You seem obsessed with him."

Burks nodded. "I am. He's like family, the wrong side, mind you. I want to visit him in prison. You too, if I can prove you helped him commit a crime."

The elevator clanked to a stop. Burks drew his pistol and opened the cage. "Get your gun out, rookie. We can talk about living arrangements for you later."

The pair of policemen walked into the massive room without an east wall where the ravenmen flew out earlier. A sailor attached a chain on the floating ship to the building as wingless ravenmen with sagging uniforms rushed off.

"Hands in the air and face the wall!" Burks shouted. "This is the police! You're all under arrest!"

The bewildered ravenmen assented to the order. Burks grabbed the shoulder of one of the ravenmen. "What's the rush? Who plucked your feathers?"

"I don't know," the ravenman replied in a surly voice. "One minute, we're up in the air, and the next worms are eatin' our wings and guns away!" The man opened his mouth to show Burks his missing front tooth. "They even ate my silver filling!"

"Okay, that's all I need to see, pal! Shut your maw!"

As they gathered the prisoners, Gerald said, "Look!"

The worms rushed over the metal chain. It burst before they reached the building. The airship floated away from the building.

Titans in mutual struggle, Secret Agent X faced off with the green-faced Fantômas. The villain had torn the uniform X borrowed from one of Fantômas' officers the secret agent had incapacitated. In a frantic race, weaponless officers and wingless ravenmen rushed to escape the onslaught of the worms below that devoured metal at a frenetic pace. They ignored the sweat pouring off the brows of the combatant pair. The singular audience was Betty Dale, wearing only a blanket over her underwear.

"Damn you, X!" Fantômas shouted. He held the secret agent's throat, struggling vainly to throttle X.

X spat blood from his disguised lips. "Whine all you like, Fantômas. I'm taking you in to receive justice!"

Fantômas pulled his fist back and brought it forward to punch X in the face. X evaded, but lost valuable footing in the battle. Fantômas pressed his advantage and punched X in the throat. An explosion of gas erupted from the agent's throat, covering the area. Betty fell unconscious as she breathed in the fumes. The sleeping gas only caused Fantômas to cough slightly. X delivered a blow to Fantômas' mid-section, pushing him to the deck. Fantômas kicked both feet at X as the secret agent rushed forward. X reeled backward as Fantômas stood and rushed toward the agent. X recovered and prepared for Fantômas' blow.

The blow never came. The wood deck collapse, and Fantômas plunged through the gap, unsupported by the metal understructure. X ran to the newly-created hole and looked down. A chain below the deck wrapped around Fantômas' neck as he fell through a hole far below in the bottom of the ship. The chain pulled tight about the villain's neck, yet did not snap. He looked up at X with hatred and defiance burning in his eyes. X saw a rope on the deck portion. He picked up the rope, gauging Fantômas' position. "Do not attempt to save me, X."

Shermah worms swarmed the deck and rushed over the chain. Fantômas gritted his teeth as the chain weakened and broke, carrying the mass of worms with it.

X held onto the rope as the rest of the deck began to fold. He rushed over the collapsing deck to grab Betty's wrist and drag her along. "Come on, Betty! We've got to get off this ship!"

"We can't make it, X!" Betty said, pointing at the distance between the building and the floating ship.

The secret agent nodded. "I need to get my ravensuit back." He headed for the steps leading below. He found his suit.

"Your wings should be eaten by now!" Betty said.

He put on the suit and rushed up to the deck. "Not yet, Betty. I coated the wings to give them some protection against the worms. Hopefully, the coating will last."

He grasped Betty around the waist and threw her over his shoulder.

He rushed toward the edge and leapt off. As the ship collapsed, a spray of splintered wood and Shermah insects flew through the air. The worms coated the wings carrying Betty and X aloft.

Betty watched as the worms ate the metal wings. "X! Your coating isn't working!" The metal disappeared before her eyes as they plunged toward the ground.

"I'm not out of tricks," X assured as he tried to stabilize their flight.

Betty watched as the worms devoured the metal, revealing wooden wings beneath. She laughed as the worms fell away from the wooden wings. "They won't eat the wood!"

X nodded. "I made some quick wooden wings and hammered the metal around them. It worked pretty well, though I'm not sure these wings will be able to help us long!"

X watched as they rushed toward the ground at an angle. He sweated, muscles straining, as he tried to control the flimsy wings. The ground was near as the wings finally collapsed under the weight and the battering air. X rolled on his back to take the brunt of the fall. Betty held onto his neck as they struck the ground hard. The air forced out of his lungs with a *whuf* as the wooden wings crumbled beneath him. Betty rolled off X once they were on the ground.

X rolled onto his side, gasping for air. A chunk of wood protruded from his chest.

Betty rushed to his side. "X! Are you okay? You have a chunk of wood stuck in your side!"

X opened his mouth, but couldn't speak. Thinking quickly, Betty removed her blanket and began tearing it into strips. She placed a piece of wood between his teeth. "Bite on this!"

X closed and opened his eyes in an attempt to maintain consciousness. He bit on the wood.

"Not going to lie to you, X," Betty said as she pulled the piece of stake out of his side. "This is going to hurt."

X grimaced at the pain, yet did not have enough air to release more than a huff.

Using the torn blanket, Betty went right to work dressing the wound in X's side. X fell into unconsciousness. When he opened his eyes again, he was in an ambulance with Burks and Gerald Dake looking over him. "I've got you solid now, pal!" Burks said through a broad smile. "You're going up the river for sure!"

Weakly, X nodded. Gerald shrugged over Burks' shoulder. "I'm sorry, X."

X shook his head. "Don't be. You did your duty and were true to your position as a police officer." X coughed blood to punctuate the statement. "Is Betty all right?"

Burks nodded. "Miss Dale is right there," X saw Betty smiling at him. "I can't prove she helped you, but she needs to go to the hospital. We got the entire force to help in the arrests of the ravenmen and the flyin' sailors. Looks like it's all over but the cryin' for you, X."

X nodded. "Yeah. Can I have a cigarette?"

Burks shrugged and pulled the cigar from his lips. "Sure, mac. Only all I have is this cigar. You can have it."

X took the cigar. "Thanks." He placed it in his mouth and took a puff. Then, he spit it at the lieutenant.

"Hey!" Burks shouted as he moved away from the projectile.

In the confusion, the secret agent ripped open the sleeve of the ravenman uniform to remove a vial. He threw this against the wall. The Shermah worms escaped, eating a skylite in the body of the ambulance. Burks drew his gun as a cloud of gas escaped X's lips. Burks and Gerald fell to the floor of the ambulance as Betty fell against her cot.

The worms ate their way to the driver's seat of the ambulance, frightening the driver and attendant. The ambulance stopped as the men opened their doors to rush away.

Removing another small vial from his jacket, X held it under Betty's nose. She woke up with a cough as he turned to Gerald. "What happened?"

"Heat activated liquid sleeping gas. I kept it in a compartment in one of my teeth. When Burks gave me the cigar, I sucked in the heated smoke to break the vial." He looked over at Burks. "The rest is history."

Picking up Betty, X looked at the mass of crawling worms as the roof disappeared. "We should get out of here. The worms won't eat us, but something could fall."

Getting out of the ambulance, X gently set Betty on the ground. Turning to Gerald, he said, "Make sure Betty gets home."

"Do you need a doctor?" Gerald asked. "Are you all right?"

The secret agent coughed. "Not right now." X turned to the cloud of dust rising from the building, now some blocks away. "Fantômas is not dead. This is just a warning. Europe is in turmoil. Soon, wings of death will block out the sun."

THE END

Duel of Pulp Giants

While I thought of writing this Secret Agent X story, I wanted the Man With a Thousand Faces to face-off with arguably the greatest villain of the era. Fantômas was a French creation in 1911. In comparison to his ruthless brutality and callousness toward human life, not even Dracula or the Phantom of the Opera could easily complete. Varney, the vampire, was a predecessor, yet Varney had a reason for wanting to brutally murder people. He was a vampire. Whatever in life truly motivated Fantômas to gleefully commit murders, thefts, and all kinds of atrocious acts; he was the most inhuman human villain around. If ever the devil took human form, it would not be too surprising of him to take the green-faced, gleeful visage of Fantômas.

Fantômas is to Secret Agent X what the Joker is to Batman. No one ever sees the face of Secret Agent X. Fantômas has a green face, which he flaunts to the world. Both are Masters of Disguise. X is dedicated to truth, justice, and the American way (if I may be bold enough to borrow the phrase). Fantômas is dedicated to self-satisfaction and outwitting the enemy. X is about protecting life. Fantômas kills with serial glee. The comparisons are endless. Suffice it to say, that if these two were operating at the same time, their schedules were destined to conflict.

The idea of soldiers that could fly seemed compelling before the development of fast and highly-maneuverable fighter planes brought the war for the air to a level unknown before. Even at that, an armed and flying man would have instant access to his skills, dexterity, and involuntary reactions not possible with a conventional plane. Limited by only his training and nerves, a man in a flying or gliding suit would be a triple-threat. A plane required a pilot; both expensive to train and damaging to lose. Even if piloting flight suits had an extreme learning curve, if it were possible to provide each man a suit it would save on costs. An air force would be only limited by the amount of trained flyers.

Fantômas attempts to exploit this fact in a last hurrah of his brilliant criminal career. He would be glorious in the attempt, or crash to the ground like Satan in Paradise Lost. A lot of people would suffer and die either way. Secret Agent X cannot allow this, and two Titans must clash.

KEVIN NOEL OLSON has written pulp adventure fiction and sundry articles for around two decades. Poems and book reviews of his have been published in the Journal of the Masonic Society, and he has also worked as a ghost writer of adventure fiction. Recently, the third book in the Tocsin Codex series of middle-grade children's novels found publication with Cornerstone Books. Kevin is working with a film producer to produce film adaptations of the books.

SECRET AGENT "X"

by Frank Shildiner

Prologue

The target rode his motorcycle without any head protection; this was an advantage for the assassin. If this could be staged to look like an accident, few would ask questions and fewer would realize the actions that would come in the future. This death was the second to last on the list; the others fell quietly with nobody questioning their deaths as anything but natural. The last had vanished years ago and appeared dead. No matter, that one was a mere tool, not a planner like the previous killings.

The placing of the children was the best touch; the boys were easily hypnotized and placed in the dip in the road that was out-of-sight of any driver. A perfect location, had he wanted to kill this man in a bloody public manner, this would be his choice place. A Thompson sub-machine gun as the target drove by, an American criminal could hope for no better place to stage an ambush.

And soon, as expected, the man who was to die appeared, driving his motorcycle far too quickly and not wearing a head covering. At the top of the dip he spotted the boys and a look of horror crossed the man's face, only his impressive reaction times enabling him quickly to swerve out of the road and avoid the two children on their bicycles. An impressive swerve, but one that sent the man off the road and caused him to be thrown over his handlebars and crash to the ground. He was very badly injured, that much was apparent from one glance; motorcycles were very dangerous to drive on the best of occasions after all....

But the assassin would not rely on injuries alone. Lifting a small bronze pipe in the shape of a spitting snake, he exhaled hard and fired a tiny sliver of wood at his target. It struck the man in the neck, a tiny pinch few would feel on the best of days, which this was not after all. The target was dead, the venom of the Empty Quarter Asp was subtle and slow acting, but guaranteed death within days of anyone not taking an antidote within hours.

The assassin vanished from the area, moving carefully through the English countryside until he met the boat waiting on the coast. A job well done, a legend was dead and the Cobra King would rise to take his place of power in the world!

Six days later, the target, one of the greatest warriors in history, passed away in an English hospital. Mourners around the world came to pay tribute to this great man who was a true legend to friend and foe alike. The man was T.E. Lawrence, better known as Lawrence of Arabia, and the true circumstances of his death were known only to a few men on the planet...including the last man on the death list. A man now known as Secret Agent X!

Agent X's supervisor, the gruff and mysterious man only known by the title of K-9, rarely requested emergency meetings. The nature of X's position was such that quick and unplanned conferences were risky and could lead to the revelation of his well-hidden identity. The rare occasions a sudden discussion was needed always were the lead-up to a terrible crisis.

Therefore it was with some trepidation that X waited by the telephone in the bare hallway of the Victorian styled mansion. The owners of the home passed away several weeks earlier and their house was due to be emptied and sold soon, with the telephone line scheduled to be disconnected later that afternoon. A perfect location for a meeting that was dangerous for Agent X and would soon lead to even greater troubles, he was sure were about to occur.

The telephone chimed only once and X picked it up without a word, waiting for the coded statement from K-9. Hearing the phrase from K-9, "...there are, in the souls of wicked men, hellish principles reigning which, presently, would kindle and flame out into hellfire."

X immediately replied, "...there is laid in the very nature of carnal men, a foundation for the torments of hell."

These were quotes from an infamous sermon from early American preacher, Jonathan Edwards. The tract apparently terrified people at the time and was an odd choice by K-9 as a recognition code between them at this time. Possibly there was a message to be found there, possibly not. Either way, it was another strange move by the enigmatic supervisor in Washington DC. Usually the recognition codes were from some of the lesser works of William Shakespeare or Christopher Marlowe, this colonial minister was a unique change in direction.

"There's been a death," K-9 stated a moment later. "Your former comrade at arms, Colonel Lawrence of the British Royal Army died today. The apparent cause of death was a driving accident. The real cause was poisoning."

Agent X felt a cold chill run down his body, already knowing where this discussion was headed, "From the venom of a supposedly legendary snake from the Empty Quarter of Arabia."

"Correct," K-9 replied, his voice sounding strained and tired. "And further information has been sent by—call them friends of mine. The two others from that time also passed away from this venom, facts that have only come to light recently."

X exhaled loudly and asked in a strangled voice, "Are you positive of this information?"

"Completely. All sources are confirmed by the highest levels. You are the only one left from that terrible time." K-9's answer was firm and positive, the statement of a man with complete faith in the facts he presented.

Agent X frowned but didn't hesitate to reply instantly, "I'll have to return to Arabia and see if they have returned. Otherwise, more than my own life is at risk. I need to leave immediately, whether my backers agree or not."

The backers in question were an anonymous group of millionaires who provided Agent X with a seemingly endless supply of money. Their interest was in protecting the world at all cost and X was their best weapon in this battle against the many evils that existed and were attempting to take power.

K-9 chuckled lightly, "Don't let it concern you in the slightest. I contacted the backers and they have all agreed to support you fully. Whatever funding you require is available. Are you planning on using any of your assistants?"

"No," X replied without thought. While he would love to have the able assistance of the beautiful Betty Dale, this was one situation he needed to head into completely alone. "Anyone attempting to help me will only end up dying a very painful death. I need to do this by myself."

"Then good luck, contact me if you require any aid." K-9 said in a rare show of human feelings. "And don't get killed."

"Thank you," X replied and returned the receiver of the telephone to its cradle. Less than five seconds later he was out the back door and in the street, heading towards his secret base in the city. Agent X had preparations to make; it was a long distance between here and the deserts of Arabia. But a good part of his mind was back in a Bedouin camp, the date 1917....

The camp was a mixed one, with several tribes all occupying a small area. Blood feuds were suspended, much to the distaste of some of the tribesmen, but this rule was rigorously enforced by some of the strongest warriors in the camp. The loose peace was tense, but absolute, major work was afoot and all were waiting to hear what would be happening next.

The man who would one day be known as Agent X arrived at the camp, disguised as a water bearer from a nearby tribe who were negotiating involvement in the coming campaign. He slipped off easily and made his way towards the center of the camp, spotting the tent he needed to enter without being seen. The entry wasn't easy; the sharp-eyed men stationed in guard around the tent were professional killers, true warriors of the desert. But a fast, quiet entry at the tent's east side was possible and took mere seconds.

Seated in the shadows, he could hear two voices speaking quietly in Arabic. The voices were vastly different, the first sounding rough, but powerful. This was a man used to command, whose very word was absolutely law, a king of sorts, it seemed. The second was quieter and cultured, a calm, controlled energy that seemed to eclipse the other in a subtle manner.

"No man can enter my tent without being caught or killed. I tell you, my friend, your foreign agent will die a sad and painful death in the attempt." The rougher voice spat out, sounding both insulted and amused at the same time.

"If he cannot, then he is not the man for us. And we will be unable to proceed to Aqaba." The second voice answered, still calm and collected, speaking as if he was discussing the weather.

The man one day known as Agent X stepped out of his corner of the tent and in his clearest American accent asked, "What would keep you from attacking that port?"

He knew Aqaba was an important port to the Turks, who were keeping the Arab tribes allied to the British on the defensive. But more importantly the man one day known as X knew that his successful entry into this tent was a test for the great mission he was here to complete. The intelligence commander that sent him stressed that without his help, the entire Arab revolt against the Ottoman Empire was in danger. And since the Turks were on the same side as the Germans, allowing the Arab Revolt to fail was a terrible risk.

His success in entering the tent was not lost on either man, both leaping to their feet in surprise and reaching for their weapons. Both relaxed when they observed their visitor was standing perfectly still and waiting for their response, realizing he was the man they requested for their special mission.

The first man was an impressive sight despite being dressed simply in white cotton robes with a red Mosul head cloth. He had large dark eyes, a sharp hooked nose and a low broad forehead that caused him to look like the image of a barbarian king from the ancient days. His black hair was streaked with grey though his age could be anywhere from 50s or beyond, yet he moved with the grace of a man far younger. An impressive individual, a desert lord who knew battle as intimately as he did a wife…of which he had twenty-eight. This man was Auda ibu Tayi, the Sheikh or Lord of the Howeitat tribe, the strongest warriors in all of Arabia. And, unsurprisingly, Auda ibu Tayi was feared as the greatest fighting man of the Howeitat.

The second man was an impressive one as well, though in a far different way. Shorter of stature, with light colored hair, a patrician nose and deep eyes that seemed filled with intelligence. He was dressed in a sandy uniform that once belonged to the British army, but was worn from the powerful desert winds. No, physically this man was not imposing. But he projected a powerful energy and control that was almost a force of nature. This was Captain T.E. Lawrence, the British liaison to Emir Faisal, a major force behind the changing Arab Revolt.

Auda ibu Tayi stared for a heartbeat at the American agent and laughed long and hard, "You have impressed me, American. A man who can enter a tent guarded by the Howeitat is worthy of my respect. Lawrence chose well."

"It is fortunate I did, my good friend. For our American cousin has a short time to be prepared for his very important duty." Lawrence stated in a soft, calm voice. "Have you ever heard of the Circle of Father Set?"

The assassin knelt before the altar of Father Set, his head lowered as the High Priest completed the rites. The hissing quality of the leader's words were familiar to his ears, he'd heard them every day since the Circle made him one of their children. He didn't remember his parents much; they'd given him up according to the others, so they weren't worth remembering anyway.

One of the lesser brother priests stepped forward, moving between the High Priest and the assassin. He was a fat man, a surprising sight in this desert fortress. But his position as a priest allowed him luxuries the assassin found unnecessary. The master of their order never spoke to any but the priests and priestesses, too far above the lesser members of Father Set's followers. This was their way since the ancient days, back in the time the Great Serpent controlled much of the Earth. A day that would return now that their enemies were all dead, the Circle forgotten to all in the world, especially with the plans he learned upon returning.

"The Master is quite pleased with you," the priest stated, waving for the assassin to rise. "Three of the four dead, you have done well."

"The fourth one, the American warrior, no longer exists." The assassin explained, having sensed the criticism in the priest's words. He spent years finding methods of killing Faisal, Auda and Lawrence, each representing a huge challenge. But with time and a willingness to do whatever was necessary, the assassin succeeded. Auda's death eleven years earlier had been his first successful assignment, a magnificent killing done as the Howeitat leader was inspecting his new palace as it was being built.

"He does," the priest replied with an edge of annoyance in his tone. "Our master, the voice of the Great and Ancient Serpent, the High Priest of our people has knowledge you do not. He wishes you to know the last one, the disruptor of our plans years ago, is alive. Do you question your Master?"

The assassin dropped to his knees and bowed his head, the symbol of supplication when a conflict with the Master occurred. "No, of course not. I was merely shocked; I searched for years for that man! There are no records he even existed."

The priest nodded, looking briefly over his shoulder at the unmoving, robe-covered High Priest. There was no change in their leader; therefore he turned back to the Circle's greatest killer of men. This man was raised to live and breathe death, a representation of the wrath of the god, Father Set. Out of all of the children stolen or bought from the many countries in which the Circle had followers; this man was the most accomplished in the arts of killing. No matter the situation, silent assassination or individual combat, this man was able to murder for the Great Snake with expertise.

"The High Priest is not displeased with your performance. But he has sources of information you do not possess. Would you wish to know more?" The Priest asked, smiling in a superior way. He knew the assassin would believe that the fact his enemy had escaped was a personal failing. This would make the killer even more determined for what was planned in the future.

"Yes!" The assassin snapped from his prone position. He looked up, his eyes full of heat and anger, the insult of this warrior's escaping his notice was too much to bear.

The priest turned and boomed out, "My friend, you may enter."

A figure entered from the rear of the chapel of Father Set, the shadows only showing that this was not a member of the Circle. The person stepped forward, his walk a crisp step, the lights along the temple walls glinting off his high and well-shined leather boots. The assassin recognized the uniform, having spent enough time among the Europeans to know something of their culture.

The newcomer was dressed in the black and silver uniform of the infamous Nazi organization, the SS. The silver skull on his peaked cap seemed to glow in the small light, a beacon that caught the eye and created an almost unearthly menace to the officer. The assassin could see he was tall, with light blonde hair, pale skin and dark blue eyes. A dueling scar ran along his left cheek and gave him an even more dangerous air.

"This is a new friend of our people, Hauptsturmfüher Erich Kessler of the National Socialist Worker's Party Schutzstaffel Ahnenerbe Department. Captain Kessler is a member of the Thule Society, an organization that wishes to bring back the great empire of Ultima Thule."

The assassin kept his face composed as he heard that statement, secretly amused by the Nazi's foolish beliefs. Ultima Thule was never an empire; it was merely a Greek term to refer to the lands of the extreme north. There was a kingdom in the north thousands of years ago, a land known as Hyperborea which had no connection to the modern Germans in any way. Additionally, the Hyperboreans were the enemies of the Circle of Father Set, showing that the High Priest was merely using these foolish and sad little men.

"I understand," the assassin replied, no hint of laughter or mocking in his voice. "How may I serve?"

"We will help each other," Kessler said, his heavy German accent grating on their ears and rendering his words difficult to understand. "I have discovered information on your enemy. His death will help my cause. Your people will help us eliminate enemies without being detected, with your legendary skill."

"By helping these heirs to Thule," the Priest said with an ironic tone, "They will help us rise once again to our true place. They recognize we are the heirs to great Acheron, the kingdom of Father Set."

"With you as our allies to the south, Germany will rise to take Europe and beyond. The old kingdoms and rulers will take control and the lesser races will serve as slaves, which is their true place." Kessler recited, his voice rising as he intoned his faith.

"Tell me how you will help us discover our enemy, the American warrior. I could find no trace of his name or existence, and I devoted much time to his death." The assassin asked, already disliking the European. The man spouted half-formed theories that had no basis in history, speaking as if he knew the ways of the ancients. But this Kessler represented a people who sought power, ones who would serve the interests of Father Set whether they realized it or not.

Kessler smiled at the assassin, an unpleasant look that made him appear less human and more beastial, "Herr Reichsfüher Himmler and Herr Gruppenfüher Heydrich have already accomplished your goals as a gift to your people. We have let certain spies, ones who we already know are traitors to the Fatherland, learn hidden details of the deaths of your former enemies. The Americans discovered after the death of Lawrence that he and your other enemies were poisoned through a lost snake venom."

The priest pushed forward, asserting himself once again, "How does that help our people?"

The assassin spoke first, "The American is a man of honor. He will view the death of his former comrades and our return as a danger to others. He will view fighting us as a duty and will return as quickly as possible."

"How can you be so sure?" The priest sneered.

The assassin looked at him and over to the silent High Priest without expression, his dark eyes hard and unfeeling. The Priest felt as if he was staring into the eyes of a deadly serpent, causing a cold chill to run down his spine. This man, their killer, possessed the eyes of Father Set himself, the Great and Ancient Snake.

"Because that's what I would do," the assassin answered and turned away from the priest. It was time to prepare for the arrival of their enemy.

The Rub' al Khali, better known to the world as the Empty Quarter is one of the most desolate regions on planet Earth. It is two hundred fifty thousand square miles of sand deserts occupied only by scorpions, rats and the occasional scrub plant. The sand dunes resembling small mountains dotted the landscape giving the whole area a strange beauty despite the deadliness of the arid land. Random tribes of Bedouins were the only human inhabitants, moving through the region though there were vast sections even they avoided. This was the location for which X was headed, a city long lost in the sand and believed by many to be a myth.

The city was called Irem of the Pillars, a location mentioned in ancient documents and tales told in hushed whispers. Some said it was a trading city cursed by God. Others said it was a land of sorcerers that fell because of their evil, twisted, arcane and demonic ways. The truth was far more horrific and frightening, and this hidden forgotten land was best left lost. But Agent X, one of the few who knew its true location, headed deeper into the Rub' al Khali.

Despite the many years separating that last trip through this region and now, the land was still as desolate and disheartening as Agent X remembered. Loading two camels with water, he traversed the distance and remembered those days back in 1917. Lawrence and Auda, two of the most amazing met he'd ever met in his life, now lost but never forgotten.

"The Circle of Father Set?" The man who was later known as Agent X repeated. He knew something of Egyptian history, their legends and lore. But he had no answer for this question. "I know Set was the God of Upper Egypt, protector of the Solar Boat of Ra every night from Apep the Serpent. He later became the symbol of evil, killer of his brother Osiris. Set was not held in the esteem of the Egyptians the way Isis and Horus were…no, nothing."

Lawrence smiled briefly and nodded once, "I should be very surprised if you would have heard of this group, my friend. They are an ancient order, a legend told to people of Arabia as a tale to frighten children. I learned of their existence while exploring the crusader castles of Ottoman Syria. A guide I utilized briefly told me some legends he learned from his grandmother, though he appeared to have believed they were similar to the assassins controlled by the Syrian Old Man of the Mountain."

Auda ibu Tayi looked murderous, a frightening sight that even caused a slight chill down the spine of X. "They are stealers of children, lower than dogs and more treacherous than the desert scorpions. They are no legends or tales for children, but murderous beasts who venture from their caves to destroy lives."

Lawrence nodded slowly in agreement, "They worship an older form of the deity, called Father Set, the Great Serpent and other such titles. They are a terrible people, followers of an ancient religion based in murder and the worship of snakes. They are our greatest danger at this juncture. We require your aid in stopping their latest grab for power."

The man who would one day be known as Agent X stared at both men, his quick mind having a great deal of trouble grasping the information. The whole explanation was something from a Talbot Mundy tale or a Penny Dreadful. Next he would learn that the leader of the Circle of Father Set was from China and, despite being a genius, could not speak a clear sentence in English.

Yet these were not men given to foolish tales, it was clear both were in earnest. And legends in this region could actually be the truth. One example was that of the infamous Old Man of the Mountain and his Assassins, a story known around the world and the subject of many adventure yarns. But X knew that a terrible man named Hassan I Sabbah formed a cult of silent killers who terrorized the Arab world for centuries. Which demonstrated that legends should not be scoffed at or ignored....

"What are their plans? And what can I do to assist you?" X asked in an even tone.

Auda ibu Tayi laughed and stepped forward, clapping X on the back, "You are a man among men, American! Many of my own people would believe I was going mad, talking of the serpent worshippers and their ways."

"You're not a man to follow fantasies, Auda ibu Tayi," X replied and knew he said the right words. The Arab warlord clapped him on the back again and smiled, waving him to a cushion near where they were standing.

"You are correct, Auda ibu Tayi does not tell silly stories before he heads to battle. But this I have learned from my friends who know better than to lie to the Howeitat. These serpents of the desert seek to return to power and have convinced the foolish Turks to provide them with gold and positions of power should their mad plot succeed!" Auda ibu Tayi intoned, his voice rising with anger.

Lawrence, seated across from X nodded once again, "Auda ibu Tayi speaks the truth. The Circle of Father Set has promised the deaths of the leaders of the rising rebellion against their power. They seek to strike immediately, murdering Emir Faisal, Auda ibu Tayi and myself within the next week. Their first attack will occur shortly, when we attack Aqaba by crossing the desert. We will be vulnerable to attack at that time, in easy reach of a knife in the back from an unknown hand."

Auda ibu Tayi leaned forward towards X, his dark skinned face flush with anger, "They do not fight as men, unless you challenge them in their

"You are a man among men, American!"

nest! You, my American friend, have been sent to us because we need a man able to cross the deadly Rub' al Khali alone and be fit to challenge the vipers in their den."

"Alone?" X asked, surprised by this revelation. Finding one spot in the middle of one of the largest deserts on the planet was a daunting, but strangely exciting prospect.

Lawrence smiled, "There is a custom among the Circle of Father Set that they cannot ignore. Any man who faces the sand alone and discovers their temple, he is tested. If he passes all the tests, they must withdraw from their planned murder."

X nodded, having learned of other secret societies with similar beliefs. The ideas often came from the ancient days, before known time, when the sword ruled the lives of all men. "I understand."

"Then understand this, "Auda ibu Tayi stated, "when you arrive you must not do any harm to any snakes or scorpions you encounter! Those animals are sacred to these vipers in the form of men. Any who kills a serpent or scorpion in their temple is a heretic and will consequently die a slow death in the heat of a sun. It is said they will provide just enough food and water to prolong the suffering for an eternity!"

"And no doubt a temple of serpent worshippers will have poisonous reptiles in great quantities. This makes the work harder, and probably a little slower," X retorted, not happy to learn this revelation. How he was meant to get past snakes and scorpions without angering these cultists was something he needed to consider.

"Fear not, my friend." Auda replied with a wide and very amused grin. "I will teach you a trick of the Howeitat, taught to me by my father's father. This will enable you to control any serpent or scorpion you encounter. Can you whistle? Good! I will teach you tonight as well as instruct you the way to cross the Run'al Khalil and seek the temple of the Set worshippers."

Lawrence stood and gave X another brief smile, "I must return to the tribal leaders and prepare for our crossing. Farewell and good luck to you. I look forward to hearing your tales of this lost city in the sand."

And so Agent X went off with the legendary warrior chief of the Howeitat, Auda ibu Tayi, learning the whistle that saved him from snakes and other creatures more times than he could name. He was one of the best teachers X ever studied under, and their brief time together was among the most memorable in an impressive life. His words on desert survival as well as fighting tricks he learned in many battles were some of the most important tools in the Agent's arsenal, ones that defeated more than a few enemies.

And Lawrence, a legend that X would always remember well. He never wanted fame, but achieved it despite his best efforts otherwise. A sad and lonely man, but great and possessing a force within him that moved mountains. Agent X only spoke with him one other time, following the events at the temple. As always, T.E. Lawrence had been quiet and calm, listening intently and absorbing every detail, saying little but every word possessing a greater meaning than even X could understand. A great man, one that would not be forgotten in this and future ages.

And as the harsh wind blew across the Empty Quarter, Agent X felt a trace of sadness at the loss of so many great men from these terrible cultists. Discovering that Auda ibu Tayi and Lawrence were victims of their assassins, especially after X defeated them in the past, caused a cold rage to encompass his whole being. This was why he took the time to become Agent X, as a means of fighting those who would kill or harm others for evil purposes. The Circle of Father Set, like many groups he defeated in the past, would discover to their cost the danger of crossing the path of Secret Agent X!

The assassin watched as the American agent approached the secret sacred lands of the Great Serpent, his body taut with rage. That this man was able to make him, the greatest killer alive, look like a fool to the priesthood of the temple—this was a humiliation the likes of which he had never received in his life and caused him to feel as if he swallowed a vial of acid.

Turning away, the assassin dropped down a secret tunnel hidden by the sand and headed back towards the temple. Brought to the temple after he won a New Year's wrestling competition for children, the priesthood trained him in the arts of death along with the many other children bought and stolen by the priesthood. Of those children, only he survived the harsh treatment and teachings of the ancient ways of the Father Set's circle of the death.

But the training didn't stop with the ancient arts the Circle held on since before recorded time. No, they sent him off to learn from other horrific masters who supported their darker aims. The Thuggees of India, the Dacoits of Burma, the Lin Kuei of China, the Secret Master of Under Detroit and more…all taught him their methods of killing others. Whether it was with guns, weapons, poison or his hands, none could stand before the assassin. He was just faster, stronger and more able than anyone alive, yet he lived in the shadow of this American!

Since his first days with the temple, the priests always told of the challenge of the American agent when they attempted to rise in power once again. According to the tales told as he trained and killed the other children in his group, the American rode out of the desert and knew how to challenge the Circle. He passed the tests and fought their champion, forcing them to give up all ambition during the Great War.

Though thwarted at that time, the Circle of Father Set did not forget the men that destroyed their latest attempt to leave the hidden desert. Sending the assassin into the world, he tracked those men down, powerful men who were surrounded by guards, yet all fell and were believed to have died by natural causes…perfect deaths, all of them….

But the assassin was not merely a killer of men, women and children' not at all! No, he was also trained in areas such as languages, disguise and investigation, all of which he used to kill Faisal, Auda and Lawrence as well as over three hundred other men, women and children deemed enemies of the Circle of Father Set. All of his searches and work revealed that the American agent was dead, having died a pathetic death from gases in France. To find that this was a ruse—a deception meant to hide the American from the world—was a failure the assassin could not accept.

The German was waiting at the end of the corridor, his brightly polished boots and medals gleaming in low light. The assassin disliked this arrogant man, a deluded foolish bully who believed his gun and uniform made him a leader. His half-formed beliefs in the mythical Ultima Thule were laughable and sad, wishful thinking by racial theorists who were more fiction writers than scientists.

"Based on your movements, I assume the American has arrived." Kessler stated, his face creased in a nasty sneer.

"Yes, he is near the outer border." The assassin said, handing Kessler back his binoculars and wishing he could stick a knife in the man's stomach as well. A slow painful death would be satisfactory for this stupid man, a joyful event to watch.

Kessler chuckled and hung the binoculars over his neck, still amused that these primitives would be of any use to the glorious Reich. They were relics, sad little men who hid in the desert and spoke of the ancient days. All knew that the true power of the world, the rulers of the Earth came from the north. The southern blood was weak, only fit for slavery.

But the Master of the Thule Society believed otherwise, speaking of an ancient race of white-skinned priest kings who were a powerful empire in their own right. Kessler believed the possibility: as a Nazi party member and believer he learned that the Aryan was the true ruler of the Earth. Therefore these men out the south must have been the lost white race's slaves, carrying on their master's legacy.

"As we wait for your enemy," Kessler stated, trying to sound amiable,. "I would wish to see more of the legacy of lost Thule. Do your people have maps that show where the grand empire's cities once lay?"

The assassin suppressed a smile, but nodded. The libraries of the Circle were extensive and did come with misleading, wishful documents of those who believed in the false land of Thule. The Nazi could have all those documents if he wished; the so-called cities of Thule were set in the middle of terrible ice-fields, treacherous mountains and in places such as the mountains of the Far East. All of the maps, scrolls, and books were amusing and ultimately worthless.

"We have a room devoted to your glorious people," the assassin replied, trying to keep from laughing as he led Kessler through the halls. The room was set aside, along with others devoted to false lands and tales that were popular among people in the world. Once a new interest in a fictional empire or form of magic rose up among the wealthier classes, the Circle of Father Set would send people out in the world with evidence to prove the truth. This almost always would result in terrible chaos, furthering the power of the Great Serpent Father Set.

They passed rooms devoted to witch hunting, demon magic, the city of El Dorado, the cult of Aten and more, before coming to the small room devoted to Ultima Thule. Some of the scrolls dated back to the time of the Greek heroes, when philosophers wrote their dreams as if they were facts. Amusing, and this room could be used to foster the theories of the Nazi madmen of Europe.

"All of these items are to be yours," the assassin said. "This will help your people return to the truth that is Ultima Thule."

Kessler rubbed his hands together, seeing how Reichsfüher Himmler would reward him for proving his beliefs to be correct. "I will want to place all of these items in special containers. Reichsfüher Himmler will wish these items to be translated immediately."

The assassin nodded, "I will order this to be done immediately. Is there anything else you require?"

Kessler picked up a gold ring that sat on a shelf, sensing it was the property of a great king. He tucked the ring into his uniform blouse; this would enable him to claim his connection to the line of kings that Himmler revered. "No, nothing. Just send a servant to tell me when the American arrives. I wish to assist in his torture."

The assassin nodded, amused that the Nazi was holding the gold ring with such reverence. This ring was merely an Egyptian forgery made from a Hyksos statue of Father Set, made to look like a crude northern relic. Leaving Kessler behind, the assassin put the Nazi fool out of his mind. The American agent was his only interest now....

The night wind howled through the Empty Quarter, a cutting wind that could kill the unprepared in minutes. Agent X tightened his head covering and leaned a little closer to his mount, grateful for the lessons he received from Auda ibu Tayi. The legendary warrior chief, though feared by many, proved one of the greatest influences in X's impressive life.

"Remember, my American friend," Auda stated as X was about to leave the camp. "Always do what you know to be right."

"Is that how you live?" The man who would be known as Agent X asked. Auda ibu Tayi, while legendary for his hospitality, was a fierce warrior who killed more men than any realized.

Auda smiled broadly, his gums visible in the twilight. It was known that when he chose to take Lawrence's side and revolt against the Ottoman Turks, his first act was to shatter his Turkish-created false teeth.

"Always!" He intoned, "Life is an epic tale, a saga of heroes and the craven. The choice of all men is whether to sail like the eagles or crawl in the dust like the jackal."

And with that, Auda ibu Tayi, clasped X's shoulder and returned to his tents. Lawrence would later write that it was only with that great warrior's influence could they gain the loyalties of the tribes to help them attack and defeat the Turks.

X rarely indulged in thoughts of the past, but Lawrence and Auda were influences he felt keenly in his chosen life. The idea that both men were executed by stealth as revenge for a cult, a terrible group that should have been forgotten or destroyed thousands of years ago, was an act of evil he could not bear. No, this would be a final reckoning with the Circle of Father Set!

Hours later, he stopped the camel and waited, hand on his gas gun. The last time he was in this area, the cult's first test appeared, seemingly out of nowhere. It was the hottest part of the day, a time when no living creature stirs in the Rub' al Khali. The camel was hunkered down under an outcropping of dune while the young American sat beneath a tiny Bedouin styled tent made from his robes.

The hardest part of this journey, he knew, but was warned by Auda, besides the incredible boredom and loneliness one feels in the deep desert, was the urge to drink. The heat and the desolate sand as far as the eye could see, caused one to feel the need to drink from your precious water supply. But to do so was a death sentence, as sure a way of dying as traveling beneath the ocean without air. The man who would one day be known as X understood this all too well, having served twice in the desert and once beneath the deepest trench of the Atlantic Ocean. The desert trips were as terrifying as entering the undersea city of the Agartha, and equally as lethal...even without the Terrorbots....

Fighting off the thirst, the Agent dozed lightly and hoped for a deeper sleep. It hadn't come in three days, but he was hopeful the prolonged time in the Rub' al Khali would allow him to become used to the overwhelming power of the desert. The Bedouins were raised in this environment and no matter how excellent their teachings, it would always be a foreign world to any but their people. But the man who would one day be Agent X knew that he had to defeat the Rub' al Khalil to save the lives of men who were fighting a war on his side.

It was a rustling sound in the nearby dune that woke him this time; usually that meant a rat was scurrying into another burrow or a soft wind was blowing across the land. The Agent opened his eyes, always on the guard even in this desolate wasteland. This time it served him well, because three men in the robes of Bedouin were creeping in his direction, curved swords in their out-stretched hands.

Staying perfectly still and breathing as if he was asleep, the Agent waited until the men were about to raise their swords when he drew the pistol at his waist and fired in one motion! The first two men fell, dead before they hit the ground, when the third threw his sword at the agent. The blade struck the pistol, shattering the barrel and forcing the Agent to drop his ruined weapon. The swordsman grabbed another blade from a fallen comrade as X leapt to his feet and scooped up the other sword.

The Agent and the robed swordsman circled each other for a moment; their eyes locked, their bodies relaxed and ready to spring. It was the cultist who acted first, screaming as he swung his sword in a fast arc towards the

Agent's neck. The Agent parried the attack with his borrowed blade, feeling the shock up his arm. Stepping back, he feinted towards the man's head and smiled slightly as the swordsman raised his blade to block. With an upward flick taught to him by a German saber maestro, the flat of the Agent's blade struck his enemy's hand. This caused the swordsman's grip to loosen and his weapon to drop to the sand. This was a classic trick used in real combat with swords, not a fencing attack like that known to most men who used weapons.

Placing the borrowed sword's point against the man's neck, the Agent waited a full minute. He needed the man to realize his position completely. One slight flick of X's wrist and his enemy would be dead in seconds. There was no method of escape at that moment; the man in Bedouin robes was completely at the Agent's mercy.

"I will let you live," the man who would be known as Agent X said in soft, calm Arabic, "if you do as I demand from you. You will tell me the location of your temple and who I must face to avert their plans."

The swordsman looked at the Agent without expression, his only movement the slow rise and fall of his chest as his breathed. His unblinking gaze remained on X, causing him to resemble one of those clever waxwork figures that Professor Henry Jarrod created back in the United States.

"Do you understand me?" X demanded, hoping these cultists did not speak another language.

The swordsman smiled and said, "I understand you. But this does not matter; Father Set will take me in his embrace."

With that, the man seemed to clench his jaw and a low crunching sound was audible to the Agent. The swordsman toppled over, his mouth filling with foam, his body convulsing and falling still in seconds. The American spy stared down at the fallen man, horrified that this group of fanatics was prepared to die for their twisted faith.

Now, years later and in the same area, nobody stirred in the darkness of the Rub' al Khalil. It appeared the crazed cultists of Father Set were not prepared to send more fanatics to their death in the same way as they did in the past. But this time Agent X would not be horrified by their terrible actions; his work since this assignment for Lawrence taught him that evil fanatics were capable of behavior that defied the imagination!

The assassin checked the tests for the third time, wishing he was not forced by tradition into waiting behind a set of traps for the unwary. If the American was as good as legend held, all three traditional methods of death would fail to destroy him and force the temple elders to agree to a duel of honor. It was a foolish method of behavior, the assassin knew all too well that you never allowed your target a chance to fight back; kill them as quickly and as easily as possible and get away unseen.

"What are you doing?" Kessler demanded, an ancient rusted sword was now in his belt and he was behaving as though the weapon was a normal part of his uniform.

The assassin suppressed an urge to snatch the sword away and jam the rusted blade into the arrogant Nazi's eyes. A jackbooted thug, that's all Kessler was, a bully who delighted in his black uniform and medals as well as his right to kick anyone he perceived as weaker. The assassin had killed three temple candidates who behaved that way back in their days of training. Three perfect murders, all performed by the time he was age eight, the precision and reason for the kills had impressed even the rarely speaking High Priest of the Temple.

But the assassin had no choice but to behave with politeness under the High Priest's orders. And one never violated the commands of the temple's master, for to do so was to invite a painful and very slow death. Even the assassin, despite his expert skills in the art of death, feared the High Priest of Father Set.

"Checking the traps used to test anyone who wishes to challenge the Circle of Father Set. Under ancient law they must face three challenges, each more terrible than the last. Then they are given the right to duel the champion of the temple." The assassin explained, keeping his voice carefully neutral. He was speaking to Kessler in German, his accent that of a Prussian noble, though the Nazi failed to realize the skill being demonstrated.

"My men and I will face him should he survive your silly and easily defeated ordeals," Kessler stated. He was standing in a pose he often used to impress Reichsfüher SS Himmler, hands on hips, chin held high, chest thrown out. Kessler knew he resembled an SS recruiting poster, which made him an ideal candidate for Himmler's attention.

"That is against the laws of the temple," the assassin replied, knowing it would do no good. But manipulating Kessler would be enjoyable sport as well.

Kessler sneered, "Pah! What do I care for your degenerate ways! We men of Thule will show you the true way of battle!"

"Truly? How will you do that, Herr Hauptsturmfüher?" The assassin asked, seeing a way to rid himself of the lot of these Germans.

Kessler's sneer widened as he looked down at this temple's so-called greatest warrior. A nothing of a man, soft-spoken and almost cringing and craven, no threat to a member of the elite SS. No doubt he earned his rank by birth instead of by deeds; such was the way of lesser folk.

"I will show you. Hauptsturmfüher Vogel, present yourself at once!" Kessler barked, looking over his shoulder to the room that held his small troop of men.

The man who stepped out from the small room was dressed only in a pair of white boxer shorts with the Nazi eagle emblazoned on one leg. He was of average height and build, with dark blonde hair, green eyes and a sneer matching the one across Kessler's face. The man's right arm shot up in a ridged salute and he cried, "Heil Hitler!"

Kessler smiled and replied with an equally flashy salute. *"Seig Heil!"* he shot back. "Hauptsturmfüher! Demonstrate how we shall destroy the American agent."

"My pleasure, sir," Vogel replied, his voice an odd low purr. Lowering himself to the stone floor, he suddenly began to shake, his muscles rippling across his body and causing him to groan in obvious pain. The air filled with an odd popping and crackling sound and a moment later it became apparent that the noise was that of Vogel's bones breaking and reforming. Fur began to sprout throughout his body, a ragged brown hair with pale spots that was very unattractive to the eyes.

The assassin watched the display without expression, but in truth he was growing bored with the spectacle. Part of him was amused as Vogel shrieked as the bones in his head started to shatter and reform, becoming narrower with a nasty, stubby snout. As one raised in the faith of the Great Ancient Serpent, the assassin was used to displays far stranger than the one before his eyes; the High Priest alone was capable of feats that would cause most men to weep with terror. Kessler's delight was slightly amusing, but rather ridiculous in the end.

"There you have it, the future of the German people as they embrace their Thule heritage!" Kessler shrieked, raising a fist in the air as the transformation was complete. He knew this was his moment of triumph, one that would earn him high rank in the SS and allow him to trample the lesser races beneath his feet.

"Werehyena," the assassin intoned, his voice lacking any emotion. A simple enough accomplishment if one knew the correct drugs and powers to use. But ultimately fairly useless since a hyena, while dangerous, was not

"My men and I will face him should he survive your silly and easily defeated ordeals," Kessler stated.

a predator capable of turning the tide in a battle. They were pack hunters and feared by many animals, but the assassin had learned from a Russian General to hunt the creatures armed with only a spear and a sword. Most werehyenas were criminals, cursed for stealing from the dead or behaving like rampaging beasts in the presence of the wrong shaman. What had Kessler and his fools done to receive the curse of becoming one of the most reviled creatures on Earth? The assassin didn't know or care truthfully; he merely found their actions an unimpressive demonstration of power.

"Correct," Kessler said, his sneer returning as four more werehyena padded out of the room. "An army of such creatures at Herr Himmler's and Herr Heydrich's disposal will be an element of terror that will cause the Fatherland's enemies to quake with fear. It will be glorious!"

"No doubt," the assassin replied, not hiding his scorn for once. Possibly these creatures could serve, there was nothing to say that a fourth test was against the rules. Either the animals would destroy the American agent or he would dispose of them and Kessler…to the assassin's mind, there was no possible means of losing in this situation.

"You have convinced me, O glorious son of the legendary Thule people," the assassin added, impressed with himself that he wasn't laughing in the Nazi's preening face. It was truly amazing how people could fool themselves into believing the most ridiculous notions.

"Yes?" Kessler asked, sounding wary. He mistrusted this silent and craven little man and doubted he was capable of good will unless ordered by his robed master, the silent High Priest.

"Yes," the assassin said, smiling and showing his teeth. "I will take you and your pack of creatures to a chamber the American must enter after completing his trials. Feel free to tear him to shreds. I will be in the main temple, awaiting news of your magnificent battle."

Kessler nodded, still mistrusting this man but accepting a chance to prove why the German was the highest and greatest of all the Earth's creatures. Hadn't he discovered the wise man in the cave in West Africa who knew how to make his men into shape-changers? Hadn't he threatened to torture the man unless he showed them the method? The fact that the wise man imparted the information easily was no surprise; he recognized true greatness.

Kessler waved the other man on, barking a quick command for his pack of soldiers in hyena form to follow. What man could stand against such terrifying might?!

Secret Agent X found the strange rock formation that jutted above the dunes, untouched by the powerful sandstorms that blanketed this region. A huge black stone at least five times the size of a man, the formation did not reflect the light, in fact the light seemed to be absorbed and consumed by this odd mineral. Was this marker of the temple of the Circle of Father Set here before these terrible cultists, or did they place this rock here as a warning to any who dare enter their lands? X did not know and doubted even the men of the Circle had the answer, just another mystery lost in the sands of time, so to speak.

Walking to the south side of the enormous boulder, Agent X began studying the glass smooth wall. After several minutes he found the symbol that Auda informed him was the marker for those who wished to enter the terrible Temple of Father Set. A tiny etching of a serpent, smaller than a thumbnail, was visible on the surface of the stone close to eye level but just low enough that the symbol would be easy to miss.

Kneeling down, X placed both hands on the rock and was once again astonished by what he felt on the smooth, glasslike surface. The stone's façade was cool to the touch…yes, cool despite the obvious fact that this obsidian colored mineral was placed openly in the fierce rays of the sun beating down on this, the harshest desert on the planet Earth.

Moving his hands slowly downward along the rock's outer face, Agent X stopped a moment later, smiling beneath his Bedouin-styled face covering. Hand-shaped indentations, invisible to the naked eye, could be felt by X, the fingers far longer and wider than even the largest human hand. Agent X placed his fingers in the approximate proper locations on the stone and gently pushed. Just as in the past, the enormous stone slid back several inches, revealing a small tunnel leading below the surface of the desert sand. How the gargantuan stone moved from so small a shove was a mystery, one X vowed once again to solve in the future.

Say what you will about the Howeitat warrior Auda ibu Tayi, his knowledge of the ways of the desert was unsurpassed. Somehow the great warrior chieftain knew the secret way of entering the hidden temple beneath the sands of the Rub' al Khali. Most men would merely provide scraps of legends of this hidden and lost temple; but not so Auda, it was no doubt a point of pride that his information was more detailed and exact.

Stepping down into the darkness, X was unsurprised to see the obsidian stone sliding back into place. Possibly a pressure button hidden in the tunnel caused this mysterious action, though given the oddities surrounding this temple, anything was possible. Reaching up to the

Bedouin headdress that he wore since entering the empty quarter, Agent X pulled down a pair of goggles he kept hidden beneath his turban. These were light-intensifying glasses, able to make even the darkest room seem well-lit to the wearer. In the event of sudden bright light, the lenses would instantly darken and protect the eyes, preventing even the normal blindness one experiences when going from dark to light.

The tunnel was a roughly carved cavern, possibly once the source of a stream of water that was connected to the long since dried up sea that was once where the Rub' al Khali now lay. The stone floor and walls were smooth and dry, cooler than the above desert, but the air possessed a fetid and stale quality that made breathing difficult. Agent X examined the ground and walls carefully, remembering with a slight shiver the last time he was in this cavern....

The man who would one day be known as Agent X stood perfectly still as the giant rock closed above him, wondering what horrors lay before him in this ancient place of evil. Auda and Lawrence warned him that the Circle of Father Set always tested anyone entering their ancient lands with lethal traps. Seeing no source of light, the American agent reached into his jacket and pulled out a small tube of cardboard and brass, flicked a lever and blinked as a small beam of light emerged from the tube. A novelty item he bought in France, this mini-torch was a good, if short termed, source of light that saved his life several times. In this case, the source of light was the only reason the Agent was not dead!

The narrow low tunnel was, for lack of a better term, infested. Covering the floor, walls and ceiling were creatures that would cause even the bravest of men to shriek with terror. Egyptian cobras and pit vipers slithered about, along with the tiny yet incredibly lethal African serpent known as the krait. Yet they were not alone, large poisonous scorpions skittered from place to place, and spiders as large as the Agent's fist slowly crept along the ceiling and walls. This was truly a nightmare, a poisonous welcome committee from the Circle of Father Set for the unwary.

But the Yank was not without weapons! Having been told by Auda ibu Tayi that the cultists venerated the serpent, and that harming such creatures would result in an instant sentence of death, the Howeitat Sheikh was prepared with a method to keep the Agent alive.

Auda looked down at the large pit viper he dropped before him, the angry reptile hissing menacingly at the chieftain. He smiled a gumless grin as X recoiled at the poisonous serpent, seeing the knife in the American agent's hand.

"Lower your weapon, American. This little one will not harm anyone." Auda stated and began to whistle. The sound was a low noise, almost a humming vibration emerging from his lips. The pit viper was immediately transfixed and stared up at the Howeitat warrior. Auda continued to emit the sound while his hand moved back and forth. The snake moved wherever the Bedouin chieftain pointed, completely under the spell of the whistling man. It was an incredible display, only stopping when Auda forced the serpent back into a large cloth bag.

"That was...unexpected..." The American managed to say.

Auda bowed, touching a hand to his chest. "A lesson from my father's father, learned from his father. An ancient skill of the desert which has served me well. Now I shall pass this on to you, my young friend."

The whistle served Agent X well back in the temple, causing the snakes and other poisonous creatures to charge ahead of him and slay several waiting warriors further down the tunnel. An excellent skill that served X many times after that date, another reason the Agent needed to deal with these madmen once and for all.

Many years later, Agent X was almost disappointed the cultists did not once again attempt to use the poisonous creatures as the first obstacle. Apparently the trials would be further along, closer to the hidden temple proper.

It was at that moment that Agent X heard a light clattering sound along the cavern. It was a strange, soft sound that grew in intensity by the second. Looking around slowly and carefully, X observed a small stream of sand falling from the ceiling and covering the stone ground. The stream was spreading and suddenly Agent X realized with horror it was increasing.

Starting to run down the tunnel, Agent X found the falling sand was blinding him more and more, causing his very breath to be difficult to draw. Within twenty feet, X knew he was barely progressing, the sand already rising past his knees and getting faster with each passing second. Agent X knew within seconds he would begin to drown in the infamous sands of the Rub' al Khali!

Erich Kessler watched his men, in their hyena forms, fan out and move into the shadows of the cavern that housed the Temple of Father Set. He hated this place, knowing these lesser creatures thought of themselves as equal to the Aryan race. Everyone knew the Viking was a German and that the Viking was the mightiest warrior in recorded history and that the Viking was the heir to the Thule Empire. To believe that lesser races were capable of building great empires like the one the Circle of Father Set believe existed was foolish and sad in Kessler's opinion.

Looking over at the silently cringing little man, Kessler smiled again. This, their great assassin, was a weak man who had no idea of true strength. "Do you know that the pyramids were built by the Thule Empire?"

The assassin looked up at the Nazi and was grateful for his training since the temple took him into their embrace. To show any flicker of emotion resulted in an immediate beating from the temple priests. Twenty children died before the assassin's eyes before he was six summers old, and later the assassin killed three others who wept later after their proper beatings. Strength was everything, to follow the Great Serpent Father Set you needed to give up all human emotions and become like the god himself. The assassin knew he was far from perfect; he still felt amusement, disgust and anger, but he hid those base emotions well enough so that even the High Priest did not even question his commitment to their faith.

"Truly?" The assassin asked Kessler, wishing to hear this latest foolish speech. The werehyenas were moving into shadows and would behave like all such lesser cursed creatures soon enough; they would attack any enemy and later any humans nearby including their commander.

Kessler nodded and looked off in the distance, "I learned this from SS Reichsfüher Himmler's personal advisor on ancient history and magic, Oberfüher Karl Maria Weisthor. Herr Weisthor has ancient powers because of his blood connections to the ancient Thule Lords that ruled the Earth 200,000 years ago. His people were teachers of the Thule after the fall of the great Empire due to the demonic forces of lesser races."

"And he stated that your Thule people created the pyramids and monuments of Egypt?" The assassin asked, knowing the true birth of Egypt through the teachings of the temple.

"Yes," Kessler replied, watching his men vanish into the shadows and slowly stop yipping like animals. These men alone would have gotten him a promotion and a medal. The books and artifacts along with the death of the American spy would earn him at least a Colonel's rank and a place on Herr Himmler's personal staff.

Kessler turned back to the assassin, hands on hips and shoulders back. It was a pose of strength he used when interrogating army and navy officers suspected of disloyalty to the Reich. They knew he was a strong man, one far above them no matter what rank pips sat on their shoulders.

"The land you call Egypt was a small city, one built to oversee the slave races of that continent. The kings and queens of so-called Egypt were lesser children of Thule, ones not worthy of the mighty kingdom. Still, they were far beyond those who inhabited that land and were worshipped as gods by the slaves." The Nazi Captain explained, seeing the past as Weisthor explained it to him before this trip. The man was a great mystic, SS Reichsfüher's personal advisor on mystic matters and one who would bring back the greatness of the Thule Empire!

The assassin nodded and merely stated, "I was not aware of that information. Thank you. Your leader Weisthor sounds like a great man."

In truth, this Weisthor was an obvious crank and fool, the assassin knew all too well. Having spent some time in disguise in Berlin, he knew that the one known as Heinrich Himmler was a lesser man who created fantasies as a means of bolstering himself and his followers to a false belief of greatness and respect. They would wear impressive uniforms and practice saluting and behave like thugs to anyone better or in a position of weakness. And in the end they would fall, their insane and silly philosophies laughed at by anyone with sense.

Kessler nodded and looked at the ring he appropriated for himself. This ring would allow him greater access and position within the SS, a place in the growing knighthood Himmler wished to create. As one of the new Teutonic knights, Erich Kessler would pay back those who held him back, the teachers and schoolmates who once scoffed at his future greatness.

"He was recognized by the SS Reichsfüher as a great man the moment they met. Herr Himmler made him a Colonel immediately and less than a year later, a Lieutenant Brigadier General. No doubt before long he will be second only to the Reichsfüher himself!" Kessler cried, his shoulders thrown back even wider, his chest out, a picture of a masterful officer of the SS.

"You will have to tell me more some day." The assassin replied, turning away to head into the temple again. He was bored with the German and his tales of fictional places and ideas, able to predict most of what the man said before the words emerged from his smug lips. "In the meantime, I must return to my duties. The American has tripped the sand traps. Two more trials before your soldiers are allowed to act. Try to encourage them to leave the head intact. The High Priest would want it for his collection."

Kessler clicked his heels and gave a sketch of a salute, "I shall do my best to accommodate." He said, secretly marveling at how savage and barbaric these cretins were and what a pleasure it will be to burn this temple to the ground as he left. But for the moment, he would act civil and attempt to teach them the errors of their ways.

Agent X fought to stand upright, knowing that losing balance meant a painful, suffocating death at the hands of these terrible murderers. Their traps were designed to destroy lives, an ancient challenge that eliminated people who wished to prevent this cult from destroying more lives. They were intentionally deadly, created by frightened, twisted cultists whose plans were so terrible they were exiled to this hidden temple in the most desolate desert on the planet.

The sand falling from the ceiling was a painful, punishing storm that buffeted X's body and threatened to crush him under its relentless weight. The Agent staggered, but forced himself to remain upright, to fall meant never rising again! In the mountains of Tibet, an elderly Sherpa taught the Agent a very simple lesson in the event of an avalanche; a sadly common occurrence if one lives in the highest mountains on Earth.

"Fall and you die," the elderly Sherpa explained, not hiding his doubt that a person from the outside world would survive in any event.

Agent X forced his leg to move forward, moving his foot a mere inch above the cavern floor, knowing a large panicked step would cause him to trip and suffocate. The sand was almost knee deep and the Agent struggled to move his leg another inch. He had at least a hundred yards to go and knew he would not make it at this rate.

But there was a possibility, a small chance that came to his mind less than a second later. Knowing the danger of sandstorms, Agent X prepared himself with a mini-breather of his own invention. A tube the size of a fountain pen, by placing it in his mouth, he would have approximately twenty minutes of air. If X allowed himself to be covered by the sand, he might be able to burrow to the cavern roof for more oxygen and a chance to escape.

The danger was two-fold: first was the sheer volume of the sand had a good chance of covering him to such a degree that his chest would be unable to move, preventing any chance breathing. The other problem was

The sand falling from the ceiling was a painful, punishing storm that threatened to crush him under its relentless weight.

this device had about twenty minutes of air, give or take a few minutes. If Agent X couldn't get to air after that time period, he would suffocate as surely as if he just sat down and let the sand cover him head to toe.

No matter, the Agent knew this was his only chance of surviving this trap and going on to fight the cultists. Continuing to move forward, the sand was already waist deep and would be past his chest in mere seconds! Bending his head forward, X pulled out the breather and quickly slammed it into his mouth. Even a second's hesitation could have lost the device or cause it to be fouled by the relentlessly falling sand. But the speed of his action was timed just right, clean air flooded into his lungs instantly and rendered him able to concentrate on what he needed to do to survive.

Curling into a ball, X used his arms to loosen the sand about his chest and face. The idea was to create a pocket of space around his body, granting some breathing room for himself and making the possibility of escaping this terrible trap a possibility. Within seconds Agent X was completely enclosed by the sand, the only sound he could hear the drumming of the fall above his body.

A moment later, the thrumming thud of the falling sand ceased, the only sound in X's ears was his own slow and labored breathing. Knowing he was on a distinct time limit, Agent X began to dig upward, slowly attempting to move his body through the sand above him. But he was unable to make any upward motion! Unlike dirt or stone, this trap gave him nothing to use as a means of propelling himself upward. The fine particles moved and gave, but seemed almost frictionless. X was trapped with no escape. What would he do to escape, or would this be revenge of the Circle of Father Set after all these years? Agent X struggled for a solution, knowing he had mere minutes of air left!

Kessler threw his head back and howled with laughter, having watched the sand trap that Agent X stumbled into. The Temple of Father Set had a clever means of monitoring their various tests for the unwary. Through the use of hidden mirrors, they were able to view areas from a distance without being seen by their victims. It was a low-technology solution, but perfectly fitting with this hidden shrine in the middle of the desert.

"This was the vaunted Agent X? The man who men in the Abwehr and the SD feared and perpetually plotted to kill? Murdered by a clan of primitives in the middle of nowhere!" Kessler howled, cackling at the idea. He would severely humiliate many high-ranking members of the military as well as the SS's intelligence service, the SD. This would be a truly enjoyable time to come; a chance to annihilate many of those looked down upon him over the last few years.

The assassin looked at the mirror for another moment and looked over at the preening Nazi buffoon. "The American will survive. He reacted wisely when he realized the sand would engulf him quickly. I doubt this will be his end."

"No man could survive that much sand covering his body! He is suffocating slowly, unless you plan on helping him escape!" Kessler snarled, touching a hand to his Luger. Was this savage preparing to betray their alliance? Erich Kessler knew non-Aryans could not be trusted to act with honor, having read and been instructed on that fact many times since joining the SS.

The assassin shook his head, long past being tired of this man and his constant need to prove superiority. He was such a little man who was determined to tread upon everyone to prove he was a worthwhile human being. "The men of the deep desert confront far worse every week in the Rub' al Khalil. This American has learned their ways from Abu ibu Tayi of the Howeitat, a man who knew the desert better than any in this lifetime."

Kessler snorted derisively, doubting lesser creatures that chose the desert of their home capable of anything of interest. "I see no movement beneath the sands; he is suffocating slowly and will die in minutes. My men and I will prepare to leave immediately. Ready your silent killers, we will depart this evening."

The assassin looked over at Kessler, his dark eyes registering no emotions at the moment. "Until the death of the American is proven, you— and the items the High Priest presented to your people,—will remain. That is the agreement you made with the Circle of Father Set."

Kessler smiled and whistled quickly, summoning his men in their hyena form. "You believe you can stop me and my men? Apologize now and I may spare your life."

The assassin smiled, his dark features almost skull-like as he observed the Nazi. Was the man that foolish? Threatening the temple's most accomplished killer as well as trusting a pack of werehyenas to follow his orders? Apparently he was. Foolish, but very amusing.

"Apologize? Is that what you demand, Captain Kessler?" The assassin asked, giving the Nazi one last chance to retract his demand.

Kessler stepped closer, hand on his Luger, "I misspoke, you pathetic savage. I meant to tell you to beg. Drop to your knees and beg. I may spare you...."

The Nazi's speech was cut off by pain in his chest, his lungs suddenly unable to provide enough air to form words. Staring downward at his own chest, Kessler's eyes widened in shock; a long knife was protruding from his chest, the blade deep within his torso.

"How?" he spluttered, barely able to form the word. It was as if all air and strength rushed from his body at that moment. Was this how those he arrested felt when he tortured them for information?

The assassin stepped forward and yanked the knife out of the Nazi's chest, cleaning the blade on the man's dark tunic. "How? A foolish question, Herr Kessler. I stabbed you; your reactions are very slow, not that of a master race. in fact. No, the correct question from you would be 'why did you stab me?' And the answer to that is I could no longer listen to your endless prattle."

Kessler reached for his Luger, but his hands seemed unable to lift the heavy pistol. The assassin stepped forward, removing the gun, his actions slow and relaxed, almost ignoring the Nazi's attempt to reach for his weapon. The assassin took Kessler by the arm, leading him several feet to edge of the chamber that contained the Nazi werehyenas milling about below.

"Oh, and before you die, Nazi, I must tell you one bit of knowledge that should torment you in your last moments. There was never a Thule Empire. We gave you dross, trash we use to incite fools into spreading chaos. Father Set will thank you when he consumes your weak spirit in the afterlife." And with that, the assassin pushed Kessler down into the chamber below.

Down below, the werehyenas stalked forward towards Erich Kessler, the scent of a weak prey with lifeblood leaking causing them to forget he was their leader. Now he was merely food....

The assassin walked away, hearing the screams of the Nazi suddenly cut off. He rarely enjoyed killing, but that act was a truly pleasurable one. Part of him hoped the American warrior would survive long enough to fall in a similar manner....

Agent X knew there was only one means of escape from this tomb of sand surrounding his body: the walls of the cavern. If he could move to the wall of the tunnel, there would be a stone surface that would allow him to force his way to the surface. The difficulty was he had less than fifteen minutes of air and this movement would shorten that supply!

But there was no other means of escape, and X would not give up; he was not able to give up under any circumstances. So long as there was the slightest drop of life in his body, he would struggle to remain alive and triumph against all odds!

Slowly he pressed towards the nearby wall, his body barely able to move through the tons of sand surrounding his body. His feet on the hard stone floor propelled him the scant inches he was able to move while X's arms strained to thrust through the sea of sand. Swimming through the frozen Arctic would be far easier than this slow swimming through the material of the Rub' al Khali. Inch by inch Agent X thrust himself forward, his legs and arms burning with the sheer exertion needed to move. He knew his breather would soon run low and then out, but he would not, could not give up!

"One step more, that's all it will take!" He told himself over and over. This was a mental fiction, a trick used to keep himself from feeling anything close to despair. By keeping his outlook positive, X's body was relaxed, even when the breather gave out a moment later.

Holding his breath and moving with the same calm relaxed motion, Agent X refused to believe he was going to die. His mission was too important for him to die in a small cavern outside the temple of humanity's greatest enemy. People such as Betty Dale relied on him to protect them, prevent the evils that attempted to rise and destroy lives from gaining ground. This was why he was Secret Agent X, and this was why he would find the wall before he passed out.

And there it was! His hands felt the wall and X forced his legs forward, a relentless force moving the tons of sand that threatened to become his tomb. His lungs burning and his vision growing hazy, X placed both hands against the cavern wall above head level and released the pair of blades secreted up his arms. The spring-loaders along his forearms fired the blades forward, a lightning strike that thrust the knives into the cavern wall.

With all the power left in his arms and shoulders, Agent X pulled himself upwards, the blades fixed in the walls and allowing him to move up and up, through the tons of sand until he broke through the surface! Gasping for breath and coughing, X collapsed as he pulled his body and legs out of the death trap conceived by the terrible cultists who followed an ancient serpent demon called Father Set.

Retracting the knives, Agent X shook out the sand from his body and greedily drank the water from the tiny canteen still attached to his belt. The larger canteen was long lost, but several more were still untouched on the camels outside the temple. If he survived, he would not die of thirst, at least.

Most men undergoing such a test of survival would be unable to perform any act other than breathing for several days. But not Agent X! No, he possessed a miraculous energy, an ability to recover from the most punishing effort within mere minutes. A brief rest and a drink, and Agent X was ready to take on the next task!

"You had no right to kill the German!" The lesser priest snarled at the kneeling assassin. The fat man paced back and forth in front of the High Priest, clearly distressed and frightened. "Do you know how that will interrupt our plans? Do you?"

"No, Lord." The assassin replied, looking up at the fat lesser priest with open loathing. "But this man was intent on betraying us. He had no intention of honoring his agreement with our temple."

"You understand nothing!" The High Priest said, his voice a low sibilant hiss. The assassin and the lesser priest both visibly started, shocked to hear their master speaking for the first time. Usually he communicated with gestures or sign language; they were all taught that the voice of the High Priest of the Great Old Serpent was only devoted to their god.

"Master?" The lesser priest asked, dropping to his knees and bowing his head. He was quaking with fear and prayed to Father Set, unable to understand what was happening now.

"Silence!" The High Priest snapped, sliding closer to both kneeling men. "Know this, you barely evolved apes, the Circle of Father Set has no need for the trappings of power. We seek chaos, the death of all human life! Your species are plagues on this world, our world before you out-bred us and stole our cities!"

The assassin stared at the High Priest and a moment later smiled and nodded his head. This made sense, death to all humanity in the name of Father Set. Chaos, the best weapon to kill all those who inhabit this world. That was what he was raised to become, a destroyer of life.

The lesser priest however, was shaking his head and rising. "No! The prophesy according the Thoth-Amon was that a man would rise, the Ring of Father set on his finger, and our people would rule the world in the name of the Great Serpent!"

The High Priest snorted, an alien sound to their ears, "Thoth-Amon was a fool, dying at the hand of a mere human with a sword. My father's father wrote that prophesy, knowing you man things would find it intoxicating. It is a lie meant to fool humans into slavery."

"Liar!" The lesser priest cried and charged the High Priest, both chubby hands above his head.

The High Priest grabbed the lesser priest by the neck, lifting him off the ground, "Look upon my face and despair as I send you to Father Set, human slave."

The High Priest threw off his robes, revealing himself for the first time to the eyes of the assassin and the lesser priest. He stood about 6 feet tall, his skin a pale green and covered in smooth scales, his eyes black slits with yellow pupils. The High Priest was one of the legendary serpent men, a race thought to be long extinct from this world.

With a flick of his wrist, the High Priest snapped the lesser priest's neck, dropping the already dead body to the ground with a dull thud. "You reacted well, my assassin. We trained you well; death to all human life."

"You misspoke, High One," the assassin said and fired the Luger at the High Priest, knocking the serpent man to the stone floor.

"What?" the serpent man groaned, his chest bleeding profusely as the assassin stepped closer, pistol in hand. "What do you mean, human?"

"You said death to all human life. Wrong. Death to all life, that is Father Set's way. Chaos. I will be his avatar. But starting with you," the assassin explained and fired the gun again, smiling as the serpent man died.

Moving onto the dais, the assassin began to ring the summoning bell. All of the priests would be mustered to kill this American and the true mission of the Circle of Father Set would begin!

Agent X slid out of the sand tunnel and into a large chamber in the natural cave formation. The temple was just beyond this cavern and X knew the next trials would be here. He studied the room, a long chamber with a deep sand-covered floor. The last time he was here, this room contained idols that fired poisonous darts, which he avoided by destroying the mechanism behind the statues with a few sticks of dynamite. The sand however was the obvious trap, something to be avoided at all cost. This was a trap, probably a pit hidden beneath the layer of sand, sure death to the unwary.

Pulling out his dart gun, Agent X fired at the high ceiling, watching the tiny silken line attached to the mini-harpoon unspool. The dart struck the cave roof and held tight. Attaching the gun to his belt, X flicked a switch on the gun and began to slowly rise above the cave. Stopping when he was several feet above the ground, Agent X pushed off the nearby wall and swung across the chamber, landing safely on the stone floor beyond the sand. Unhooking the dart gun, he left it on the ground in case a quick escape was required.

Just then a hissing sound to his right caused him to freeze in place. The sound was loud, louder than that of a forty foot anaconda he was once forced to kill in Bolivia. Looking out of the corner of his eye, Agent X spotted a sight that would cause the blood to freeze in even the bravest of men!

The serpent rising from the right side of the hall was in the shape of a cobra, the same hooded and elongated head one expected to see from this legendary poisonous reptile. This one was enormous, however, the head of the serpent alone was twice the size of Agent X! It slid forward, the great snake's forked tongue as long as X's leg, hissing with anger at this intruder into its den.

Moving only his lips, Agent X began to whistle, the snake-controlling sound taught to him by Auda all those years ago. Would it control this legendary beast? Or was it too weak to control the largest snake that ever existed on Earth?!

"The High Priest has granted me control of the temple." The assassin explained to the six men and five women who made up the Circle of Father Set. The serpent man's body and that of the fat lesser priest were dropped down a nearby pit, food for the vermin now. "Gather all weapons; we go to kill the American who defies our faith."

"That is not our way," the other lesser priest of the temple stated, stepping forward. "The American must pass the three trials. Then he is granted the right to turn us aside from our mission. That is the way of Father Set."

The assassin shot the lesser priest and stepped over the body, "Ways change. Prepare for battle or I shall kill you myself."

The ten remaining members of the temple backed away with fear, knowing this man was capable of delivering death to any who stood in his way. Better to face one American and then flee into the desert than challenge the temple's greatest killer!

The giant cobra froze in place, the enormous forked tongue tasting the air but no longer moving to attack. It seemed Auda's great gift saved Agent X again! But the Agent knew this giant snake was too dangerous to merely leave behind in this chamber. No, this creature could be a means of destroying the terrible cult that lay within the chambers ahead!

X continued to whistle, flicking his hand out towards the wide doorway that led into the temple proper. The enormous snake hissed and slid forward, its gigantic body taking a full minute to pass through the doorway. The creature hissed an angry warning and suddenly shot forward, out of Agent X's sight. He heard the howl of an animal, then the snarls and howls of a pack, moving towards the giant snake with incredible speed.

Looking within, Agent X was shocked to see the great snake locked in combat with a pack of oversized hyenas! The doglike animals were snarling and attempting to find a vulnerable spot on the giant snake. The presence of hyenas was a surprise—they had no place in these lands—but that was unimportant. For now, both hyenas and snake were engaged with each other and X could move forward to destroy this temple once and for all.

Edging around the terrible battle, X entered the next room in the temple. It was a large chapel room with a statue of a giant snake circling the Earth on the far dais. Ten robed cultists stood in the room, swords and knives in hand, watching as he entered the hall.

"For Father Set!" one of the women screamed and all raised their weapons and charged Agent X as a body.

But the Agent was ready for them, far better trained than any present. Pulling out his gas gun, he fired at the running cultists and stepped back as they each began to fall to the stone floor. X stepped over the fallen bodies, knowing these men and women were the source of many deaths and kidnappings over the years. Innocents he would attempt to save, but these terrible men and women were responsible for more evil than any knew. No, destruction of this temple was essential for the good of all life.

"Well done, American." The assassin said, stepping out from behind the statue of Father Set. He had a battered scimitar in one hand and the Luger in the other. "I had hoped you were wise enough to avoid wasting time on those weaklings."

"That sword," X said, immediately recognizing the weapon. "That was Auda ibu Tayi's favorite."

The assassin nodded, clearly pleased, "I took it from him when I poisoned him to death. A perfect assassination."

Agent X felt a wave of anger fill him, a feeling he immediately suppressed. Fighting filled with rage led to mistakes, something he could not afford now. "Did you kill Lawrence as well?"

The assassin nodded again. "Another magnificent death. Now, American, I would know your name. The one you used in your country's records was obviously false."

X shook his head. "I have no name now. Men call me X, but that's just another identity I use."

The assassin bowed. "Then we are alike, for I have no name as well. Now, we shall fight. If you agree to throw aside the guns you are carrying, we will meet in honorable combat, warrior to warrior."

"Agreed," Agent X replied and tossed aside his gas gun.

The assassin tossed aside the Luger and raised the ancient sword, stalking X slowly and carefully. He was a methodical, patient killer, knowing that charging this man would be a mistake. Seeing the American had no weapon visible, he slid forward and swung for X's legs, expecting the agent to leap over the blade. A leap seemed a clever move, but in fact left the jumper vulnerable to attack once he landed.

But X was too well trained to fall for such an amateur mistake. Extending the blades hidden up his forearms, he deflected the sword attack and slid underneath the weapon. His foot immediately shot out and hit the assassin's wrist, sending Auda's ancient sword sailing out of his grasp. The assassin did not cry out, but instead pulled out the knife he used on Kessler earlier that day.

"That was all you could do? Disarm me? Perhaps you will not be a challenge," the assassin stated, circling again.

Suddenly, he feinted towards X's legs again, switched hands with the knife and slashed the Agent's arm. The blade spun out of Agent's X's hand and he felt blood begin to drip from the wound. The assassin smiled, seeing the blood fall to the floor. This would weaken his enemy and death would soon follow such a pleasure.

X immediately attacked with his knife, slashing out towards the man's free arm. The assassin was just out of reach, but was instantly inside the Agent's guard, delivering a quick slice to the cheek. He was fast, the fastest man X ever fought, and a true expert with knives.

"You are an excellent fighter, Agent X," the assassin said, his voice sounding very amused, "But you are not so good as I. I was trained from birth to be the best with any weapon."

"Interesting. I was trained to be the best at something as well." Agent X stated, standing flat-footed before this killer. This was a dangerous position, but he had an idea.

"Oh? Please tell me your expertise before I take your life." The assassin stated, seeing the American was too weak to fight much longer.

X threw the blade at the assassin's neck, knowing the man would deflect the attack with his knife. He quickly stepped forward, his rear leg pistoning out and striking the assassin in the exposed groin. The assassin shrieked and pitched forward in agony. Agent X swung the same leg up, his knee hit the man in the exposed torso as his fists raised and struck both of the assassin's collarbones. These bones took a mere fifty pounds of pressure to break and the force Agent X brought to bear was more than enough to shatter his target.

The assassin dropped to the floor, both of his arms unable to move, his nose and cheekbones broken. He could barely see and he felt several teeth fall from his bleeding mouth. X pushed the man aside and walked across the room, picking up Auda's sword and placing the ancient weapon in his belt.

"My expertise," X said, pulling out a small box from his robes, "is fighting without weapons."

He crossed in front of the battered assassin and opened the box, manipulating something and placing the item on the top of the statue of Father Set. The assassin watched him but was unable to speak; his mouth didn't seem to be able to move.

Agent X headed for the door and looked back at the fallen murderer., "That is a special transmitter of my own design. Right now a squadron of British bombers is taking to the air headed in this direction. They plan on carpet bombing the entire area. You see, executing one of their national heroes, Colonel Lawrence, was not your wisest move. But it will be your last."

And with that X left the temple to its fate, heading for the lands of the Howeitat to return the sword of the man who saved his life through his lessons....

THE END

Real People Make It Harder

One of the great challenges for any writer is to use real people in their fiction. You always wonder, in your heart of hearts, if you're doing justice to the person you're using in your tale. The closest I've come to approaching this writer's mountain is using infamous Tong leader Mock Duck in my Ravenwood tale for Airship 27's publication. In that case I wasn't hampered by anything, Mock Duck was a horrific man who caused two huge gang wars and I made fictional changes to him to make him a sinister character on the side of Frederick Brown's heroic Ravenwood. I had no need to portray him heroically or realistically then, I was writing an occult adventure that kept the terrible side of the man, while adding a dark mystic edge.

In this case I've saddled myself with two historical figures, both very heroic, and put them in a fictional situation. The first is legendary World War One guerilla leader Lt. Colonel T.E. Lawrence, a.k.a. Lawrence of Arabia. Lawrence was an incredible, if unusual individual who was far less fond of fame than most realized. Made famous by American journalist Lowell Thomas, it was often said Lawrence "backed his way into fame" and was an intensely private person who once refused a knighthood for his war activities. His work, *The Seven Pillars of Wisdom,* tells his view of the Arab revolt and remains an incredible read to this day. His death by a motorcycle accident was true and considered a national tragedy and did lead to laws requiring helmets for riders.

The other legend was Auda ibu Tayi, the leader of the Howeitat Bedouin clan and considered the most dangerous warrior in the Arab world. Lawrence stated that Auda had twenty-eight wives and was reputed to have killed seventy-five men by his own hand by the time he joined the Arab revolt. The wonderful David Lean epic film, *Lawrence of Arabia,* portrayed him greedier than any historical version and also left out his often impressive tactical mind. But like all fiction, including mine, this was creative license.

The rest of the characters were fictional, of course. Secret Agent X did use that whistle to control snakes and insects and for many years I've wanted to show the origin of that skill. Having Auda teach that to him felt right, the legendary warrior was said to live his life like a hero in an epic tale. Past writers have mentioned X worked for Lawrence in a secret intelligence mission, so I was glad to step in and make that meeting a reality.

The lost empire of Acheron was a creation of the Grandmaster of Sword and Sorcery fiction, Robert E. Howard. First mentioned in the one Conan novel *The Hour of the Dragon*, this was one of Howard's most exciting stories and remains a pleasure to this day. Why nobody has ever attempted to make this into a Conan movie is beyond me, but I'm a writer, not a soothsayer.

The martial arts used by X is based on reality as well. In addition to being a writer, I teach Mixed Martial Arts at Amorosi's Mixed Martial Arts in New Jersey under Shihan James Amorosi. Master Amorosi created his own system of martial arts and is unquestionably one of the best people I've ever known in my life. I'm continually honored to train under him and his lessons have shaped me into a far better person spiritually, mentally and physically.

All I can say now is what I always say to my readers: I hope you had a good time!

FRANK SCHILDINER has been a pulp fan since a friend gave him a gift of Philip Jose Farmer's *Tarzan Alive*. Since that time he has published articles on Hellboy, the Frankenstein films, Dark Shadows and the television's Lovecraftian links. He is a contributor to the fictional series *Tales of the Shadowmen* and has been published in *Secret Agent "X" Volume 3* and *Ravenwood, Stepson of Mystery* by Airship27. Frank works as a martial arts instructor at Amorosi's Mixed Martial Arts. He resides in New Jersey with his wife, Gail, who is his top supporter.

X AGAIN!

At long last, here we are with our fourth Secret Agent X book! I feel we do need to apologize to our loyal readers who picked up the first three volumes in this series for having to wait so long for another. Sometimes things just get away from all of us and do keep in mind, there have been several major changes in our operations and marketing procedures here at Airship 27 Productions over the past year. All of which have conspired to keep this particular title on the back shelf while other projects needed priority attention.

Well, now they've been seen to and it's time to delve once again into the incredibly exciting adventures of pulpdom's first and foremost secret agent, The Man of a Thousand Faces. I confessed years ago when we began this series that this character was one of my personal favorites among all the classic pulp heroes of the '30s and that remains true to this day. There is something about this mysterious individual that easily lends itself to all manner of stories as is clearly evident in this new collection, which, by the way, has three returning X writers coming back for another crack at him and introduces a brand new scribe to the team.

That new writer is no novice to writing pulp, in fact he is easily the most recognized of the quartet here assembled, Mr. Bobby Nash. Bobby wrote his story several years ago and has been the most patient of all our Airship 27 creators in waiting to see it in print. It's a grand tale of X facing off against a rather different kind of foe, a real-life monster. Then we follow up Jarrod Courtemanche, Kevin Noel Olson and Frank Schildiner. This is their second venture into X's world and they truly pulled out all the stops. Jarrod has him taking on an iconic Nazi mad scientist, while Kevin pits him against the notorious Fantômas, a classic French pulp character from the '30s; it's a truly suspenseful contest between these two amazing fictional characters.

And finally, our pal Frank Schildiner gives us a rare peek in X's past as he fights along side one of history's most flamboyant figures, T.H. Lawrence; better known as Lawrence of Arabia. Here's a fast paced action yarn set in the exotic and deadly world of the Saharan desert and includes the memorable scene that inspired our gorgeous cover for this issue.

Indeed, Secret Agent X is back and if you are just now being introduced to him, might I humbly suggest you go and pick up the first three volumes in this series. You'll find ads for them at the back of this book. And if you become, like me, a fan of this hero, you might want to check out the magnificent Altus Press series which collects all of the original Secret Agent X adventures, most of them written by his creator, Paul Chadwick. Honestly, you just can't have enough of a great pulp hero. Ever.

Thanks ever for your support of our efforts, do drop us a line and let us know your thoughts on this or any of our pulp novels and anthologies. And if, after reading this volume, you want more Secret Agent X tales, let us know. Believe me, you won't have to twist my arm. We invite you to visit our new on-line catalog site: (www.airship27hangar.com)

Ron Fortier
2/19/2012
(Airship27@comcast.net)
(www.Airship27.com)

Airship

Situated in the rural back country of Edwardian England is an old, mysterious house whose unique owner earns his living as a Spirit-Breaker, a hunter of ghosts. A former military veteran, Sgt. Roman Janus has devoted his life to aid those haunted, both emotionally and physically by obsessive wraiths whose spirits are still anchored to our world.

Airship 27 Productions is thrilled to present *Sgt. Janus – Spirit Breaker* by Jim Beard. Part detective, part occultist, Janus is himself a man of mystery whose own past is shrouded and the motivations behind his calling kept hidden. Within this volume you will find eight tales as narrated by his clients, each with his or her own perspective on this uncanny hero and his amazing career. Filled with suspense, terror and agonizing pathos, each a solid mesmerizing journey into the unknown world beyond.

THE RETURN OF PULP FICTION'S GREATEST SPY!

Secret Agent X, the original super-spy, is back in these three stellar collections. Written by today's best New Pulp Writers, the Man of a Thousand Faces once again defends America from all manner of evil threats.

Arguably the most popular character at Airship 27, here are the first three exciting installments in the Anthology series. Welcome to the daring exploits of pulpdom's original super-spy as brought to you by Airship 27 Productions!

www.ingramcontent.com/pod-product-compliance
Lightning Source LLC
Chambersburg PA
CBHW071239250626
47163CB00001B/245